By Colby Rodowsky

Not Quite a Stranger

Not Quite a Stranger

Colby Rodowsky

FARRAR STRAUS GIROUX / NEW YORK

Library of Congress Cataloging-in-Publication Data
Rodowsky, Colby F.
Not quite a stranger / Colby Rodowsky.— 1st ed.
    p.   cm.
Summary: After his mother dies, seventeen-year-old Zach travels from
Ohio to Baltimore, Maryland, to find the father he has never met, and
chapters alternating between Zach and his half-sister describe how the
members of the family adjust.
ISBN 0-374-35548-7
[1. Family life—Fiction.   2. Brothers and sisters—Fiction.]   I. Title.

PZ7.R6185 Nr 2003
[Fic]—dc21

2002035422

To our newest grandchild, Frances Chunju O'Connor, who comes to her parents and her extended family from Anhui province in China. Welcome.

Not Quite a Stranger

Tottie

All over the city this morning, perfect strangers were treated to an account of our recent family weekend in Williamsburg. I know this because as soon as I got to school, even before I dumped my books in my locker or had a chance to ask if anybody else'd had trouble with the math homework, my friend Ellen said, "You never told us you barfed in the car on the way to Virginia!"

"I didn't exactly," I said. "It was more like gagging. And that was only because Brian did it first, all down the back of the front seat. Which was totally gross." Brian is my seven-year-old brother and has been known to be gross even when he's not barfing.

"And that your father had to stop on the side of the

road and clean the inside of the car with bottled water and scrunched-up newspaper," said Margaret. "And that you had to ride the whole rest of the way with all the windows open."

"*Or*, that you made the bed in the motel and your mother had to tell you to unmake it because you don't need to do that in motels," said Amy. "And that you said you knew that, but if you were a maid you'd want *everyone* to make her bed. All you told us was about colonial costumes and candlelight tours."

I let out a sigh that was more of a moan. "She's done it again, huh?"

The three of them nodded in a way that let me know they felt really sorry for me—but were also enjoying this all just a little bit. "She didn't *tell* you? You didn't *see* it?"

"Nuh-uh," I said, shaking my head. The *she* here is my mother and the *it* is a piece she'd apparently written for the local paper. But I guess I'd better back up a bit and explain. My name is Tottie (Charlotte, actually) Flannigan and I live with my brother, my parents, a dog, and a cat in a big old three-story house in Baltimore. Brian is a little brother straight out of central casting. The dog, a Dalmatian named Punch, is sweet and goofy and not what you'd call a deep thinker. Erlich the cat is lovable, and nice, and unexceptional.

My father, on the other hand, *is* exceptional. He's big and burly with flame-red hair that is dense and wiry, and a nose that can only be described as prominent. His full name is Dr. David Edward Flannigan and he's what I guess you'd call a high-profile person. That's mostly because he's a pediatrician and lots of times, when we're out someplace, little kids come running up to him and yell, "Hi, Dr. Flannigan, want to see where my sore throat used to be?" (Or something equally dumb.) He's also written a book called *Kids First*, where he talks about how most of the problems kids have are brought on by their parents. Since the book came out, he's been invited to speak at a bunch of medical conventions and even local PTA meetings.

If my father is high-profile, I guess you'd have to say my mother is pretty much in-your-face. Which she literally is three mornings a week when her column appears in *The Sun*. There is a little picture of her that runs right next to the heading "Musings," which doesn't tell you much except that she's nice-looking in a mother sort of way. Underneath the picture, in not so big letters, is her name: Winnie Flannigan.

"Musings" is supposed to be my mother's thoughts and opinions about things like politics and sports and life in general. The problem is that Mom seems to have more thoughts and opinions about our *family* than about anything else. This leads to my feeling that I've been hung out for all the world to see, like underwear on a clothesline.

The thing is, my high-profile parents managed to produce an ordinary kind of daughter, one who really takes exception to forever turning up in the morning paper, along with "Dear Abby" and the comics. I mean, does the world really need to know in excruciating detail how I, Tottie Flannigan, age thirteen, reacted when I got my braces or when our soccer team lost the championship by one point? Or how I felt when my grandma died. Does the reading public really *care*?

"Of course it does," my mother always says when I ask that question of her. And then she laughs, but not in a ha-ha gotcha kind of way. She laughs a warm, rolling, all-inclusive laugh, then does something totally out of line like tweak me on the nose or blow a kiss while saying, "These are all universal truths, Tottie. The world in a microcosm. Besides, your brother doesn't mind."

She's right. Brian *doesn't* mind, but I'm firmly convinced that that's because he doesn't have enough sense *to* mind. *And*, none of his friends are old enough to read the paper. Besides, I'm sure that anyone who kept my brother supplied with food and computer games (which my mother does) would rank up there with Joan of Arc and Sacagawea. In his mind, at least.

"Didn't she? Tell you, I mean," said Ellen, yanking me back to the present.

I shook my head and sighed, saying, "Living with my family is a trial and a tribulation."

Ellen and Margaret nodded, and Amy said, "Yeah, I guess, except that your mom and dad really are the perfect parents."

"As long as you're not related to them," I said, slamming my locker for emphasis. "Come on, let's go."

We had hardly made it three feet down the hall when Billy Taggert and his gang of goons caught up with us, all making barfing noises while laugh-a-minute Billy called out, "Remind me not to take any car trips with you, Flannigan."

"How was your day?" my mother asked, once I had dropped my backpack in the front hall and had come into the kitchen where she and Brian were sitting at the table.

"Great, Mom. Really all-time spectacular," I said, pouring myself a glass of milk. "I mean, Billy Taggert fake-puked in the hall when he saw me, and Mrs. Hanson, the librarian, asked me right out loud for everyone to hear if my stomach had settled down enough for me to enjoy Williamsburg. And then in social studies, Mr. Miller launched into a whole long thing about colonial restorations and Williamsburg and ended up saying, 'Is there anything you'd like to add, Tottie?' So some kid in the last row whose name I don't even know yelled out, 'Ask her about the trip down.' But other than that it was pretty uneventful."

"But Tottie," my mother said, with the beginning of that all-inclusive laugh, "these things happen to everyone."

"Yeah, I know. The world in a microcosm. But you could at least have *warned* me."

"But the paper was right here on the table the whole time you were eating breakfast. If you chose not to read it, then what—"

"Yeah, but I was running late," I said.

"Forewarned is forearmed," said Mom, still with the hint of a laugh. "But I'm sorry if the column bothered you today."

"I don't see why you just can't write a *novel* like regular writers do," I said, and turned to look at my brother, who was prying an Oreo apart and dipping the pieces in milk. "You should pay attention to these things, too," I said, leaning close to him. "You're the one who actually threw up on the back of the front seat. Don't you *care* if people know that?"

Brian shrugged and reached for another cookie.

Zachary

It's pretty much of a crock to say I thought we'd get used to it, but in a half-baked way that's what Mom and I did think. Until we figured out, not quite at the same time, that the Big C's one of those things you don't *get* used to.

It's just there. Cancer. Gobbling up not just my mother's liver, and her life, but my life, too. At least as I'd always known it. Then it started in on the future, making chicken feed out of the law degree she was working toward, as well as her dream that when I was a senior I'd get that acceptance letter from the University of Notre Dame—complete with a boatload of financial aid. Those were the biggies and they were gone, along with a bunch of dumb stuff, too. Like the used car we'd been saving for, and the trip we were going to take to Mount Rushmore some-day—for no reason other than that we couldn't quite be-lieve it was *there* and needed to see for ourselves.

I guess in fairness I'd have to say we were prepared from the get-go. That's because no doctor worth his salt craps around when it comes to a single mother with a teenage son and no relatives within a radius of forever. And Dr. Snelling is definitely worth his salt. "I'm not go-ing to lie to you, Ms. Pearce," he said. "Or to you either, Zach. We are dealing with a very serious situation."

We? As if he were suddenly a part of the *we* that Mom and I had been for seventeen years.

I think it was Mom who first got the clue that things were going faster than we'd thought they would. That they were actually spiraling downward, outpacing the way this disease was meant to run its course. At least ac-cording to the gospel of Dr. Snelling.

I could tell it by Mom's eyes. And by a grim kind of ac-ceptance that wrapped around her and made me feel that she'd already taken a step away.

At the beginning, when the diagnosis was new and raw and totally unreal, my mother was full of plans. Back then, when she was still reading her casebooks for law school and talking about "beating this thing," she had one of the lawyers in the firm where she worked as a paralegal draw up a will. "There's nothing to leave, Zach. But it's all yours," she said. "I'd always meant for there to be more—both time and money. Anyway, it's a formality, and it's done."

Mom told me more about my father, in those few weeks, than she ever had before. More than I'd ever wanted to know. And even then, as she spoke, I tried to shut down my ears, staring hard at the water pitcher and the row of medicine bottles on the bedside table, instead of listening.

"He's a good man, Zach. A very good man."

That phrase, out of all she said, caught at my consciousness, and I fired back, "If he was such a good man, why didn't you marry him?"

"There wasn't any spark," my mother said. "We weren't simpatico."

I wasn't *spark* enough? I wanted to shout. I wasn't spark *enough*?

We didn't talk about my father anymore. Instead, Mom forced herself to sit at the computer one day, where she typed it all out—name, rank, and serial number, as it were. She printed it and sealed it in a long envelope and hobbled back to bed. Later that day she asked for a cup of tea, and when I brought it, she handed me the envelope.

"It's all in here, Zach. Your father's name and address

and telephone number and how to get there. Everything. I was never sure why I kept track of his whereabouts. Maybe in case . . . if you ever . . . And I need you to promise me that you'll go."

It was as if what hadn't actually been real now suddenly *was*, and I sat staring at the cup of untouched tea, not answering her.

"I'm going to call him, when the time gets closer," she said. "But meanwhile, I need for you to promise."

And I did, because she was my mother and she was dying and it was all I had to give her.

Mom never made that call. Before she could get to it, the Big C took its final spiral—all the way down. She slept; she woke; she was in and out of a coma, finally more in than out.

The hospice people came and went and came again. My mother's friend Sara brought meals for me and sat by the bed, stroking Mom's arm. Other friends called or stopped by, and a minister, maybe because of the hospice people, suddenly had become a part of our lives.

When my mother died, the partners at the firm where she worked asked if they could take care of the funeral, and I said yes. The minister was there again—in charge, I guess you'd say. A bunch of Mom's friends came, and Mr. Reynolds, our landlord, and a crowd of guys from school, the hospice nurse, and the old couple next door who brought over ginger cookies every Christmas.

The day after the funeral, Sara came and helped me go through my mother's things. We packed them all in plastic leaf bags and took them to Goodwill. Afterward, we picked up subs and ate them in our kitchen, and Sara asked if I wanted to stay with her family till I left to go to my father's.

I said thanks but no thanks. Said that my friend Tony's mother had asked me to stay there awhile. Then, later that night, when Tony's mom called, I told her I was going to Sara's.

I figured I could hang on at the apartment, at least until the rent was used up. One of the lawyers at the firm called "to talk finances," as he put it. He said my mom hadn't had much, what with being sick and all, but after he took care of the remaining bills he'd send what was left to me. And did I need money to get to my father's?

I said no and went, that day, and emptied my bank account.

The thing was, I hadn't yet been able to face up to the fact that my mom was gone. I needed time.

It doesn't always work that what you need is what you

get, though, because after only eight days Mr. Reynolds showed up at my door. He was an okay guy and through the years we'd talked a lot of baseball. Once, when I was eight, he even took me to a Reds game. Anyway, I asked him in and cleared my books off the couch so he could sit down.

"Look, Zach, I don't want to make any trouble, but I know you've been up here by yourself and I can't, in good conscience, let it go on. I had to call Social Services today and let them know what's what—and they're going to have someone here tomorrow afternoon around the time you get home from school. They're good people and they'll help you sort things out."

"Yeah, well, I'm heading for my father's," I said. "Soon's I can get stuff finished here."

"They can help you with that," Mr. Reynolds said. "Maybe even put you in a foster home till your dad can come for you." He tugged on one ear and then the other before saying, "There're a lot of good people out there, just ready to help."

"Yeah, Mr. Reynolds, I'm sure there are. And thanks," I said as I showed him to the door.

Thanks for nothing, I thought as I heard him go down the stairs. *Thanks for a heap of nothing.*

The next morning I left at the regular time, with no

books and my backpack stuffed with as many clothes as would fit. I couldn't risk Mr. Reynolds seeing me go out with even a duffel bag. Couldn't risk having him sic the Social Services people on me before I could get away.

When I got to school, I went to my first three classes, strictly business as usual. After that, I headed for the library, scouting out a table in the far corner and settling down to read my mother's letter. I read it again, and then again, until I could feel it beginning to burn into my brain.

Eventually someone came and sat at my table, and I got up and left, walking down the long hall at the end of the library, past the chem lab and the lockers. I stopped to get a soda from a machine before heading out the door and turning in the direction of the bus station.

Tottie

"Okay, Tottie, I want you to start waking up," my father said as he poked his head around my bedroom door on Saturday morning.

"Uh-uh," I mumbled, rolling over and burying my face in my pillow.

"I want you to start waking up *now*. Your mother's at the health club, and I'll be leaving for the office in a few minutes, and I need you awake so you can listen for Brian till she gets back."

"Yeah, uh-huh," I said, pulling the covers over my head. "I can hear him."

"I need you *up* and listening," said Dad. "I'll put a bagel in the toaster oven for you, so come on down."

"Chocolate chip," I called as I heard him start down

the hall. Then, "Chocolate chip" again, before he could tell me that wheat would be better for me. Or sunflower seed. I lay there another minute till I heard my father stop halfway down the stairs, the way he does when he wants to hear if I'm up yet. I sat on the edge of the bed for a minute and banged my feet against the floor. "Okay?" I yelled as I headed into the bathroom.

When I got downstairs, the bagel was just the way I liked it—crusty on the edges with the chocolate chips all melted inside. I slathered it with lite cream cheese (everything in our house is lite or no-fat or low-fat, mostly because my mother's a ranking member of the food police) and poured a glass of orange juice and sat down. "Thanks," I said. "For the bagel, not for waking me up."

"Sorry, Tottie, but I've seen too many kids brought into the office because of an accident that happened while someone was supposedly watching or listening for them."

"I know, and 'it only takes a minute,' " I said to keep him from saying what he always says. "But Brian's not even awake yet."

"Then you won't have much to do, will you?" he said. "Oh, by the way, your mother left this here for you. It's a copy of her column that's going to run in tomorrow's paper. She was a little concerned that *you* were concerned yesterday."

I took the pages he held out to me and skimmed them

quickly to make sure my name wasn't there, and it wasn't. Then I went back and read all the way through about how my parents were trying to find some furniture store way out in the country one day and were hideously lost and kept going back and forth over the same bridge and my father wouldn't ask for directions. "See—that's exactly what I mean," I said. "Mom's writing about you never wanting to stop and ask the way when we're going some-place. Don't you *care*?"

Dad laughed and leaned back in his chair so that the sunlight made his hair look even more like a flame. "But she's right—I *hate* to ask directions. All men do. That's what makes it so universal." He looked at me as if it was my turn to say something, and when I didn't he went on. "Come on, it's *funny*. Why, all over Baltimore people are going to be reading that tomorrow and saying, 'Just like our family.' Besides, you know your mother would never invade our privacy. These are all superficial things."

"Yeah, right. Me barfing in the car is superficial? And that trip to the bathing-suit store last summer? And the bit about me wanting to go to sleep-away camp and then not wanting to go and ending up breaking my arm and not being *able* to go? That's all superficial?"

"Well, maybe *superficial* wasn't the right word. But these aren't terribly *personal* things."

"Me trying on that bikini and Mom saying I couldn't have it was personal," I said.

"Okay," said Dad, getting up from the table. "Maybe a little personal, but the thing is, your mother writes with such empathy, such love that you know she'd hate to think of your taking offense. I have to head into the office now, but why don't you *talk* to her about this, let her know how you feel. Maybe this afternoon, while Brian's at the Y for swimming."

"I *have*, and it doesn't do any good."

"I said *talk*, Tottie. Not *attack*. A real conversation, okay?" He kissed me on the forehead and went out the back door.

I sat there for a few minutes after my father left, staring at the bagel plate and trying to decide if I wanted cereal now. I did, and got up and shook out a bowlful of Cheerios, added milk, and sat back down at the table, eating and thinking. The thing is, I gripe about Mom's column all the time, but my mother herself is actually okay, pretty cool even, except when she tries to be and then she's embarrassing.

Sometimes, when I'm at one of my friends' houses, I play this game with myself where I pretend that the house I'm visiting is *my* house, and that the mother who lives there is really *my* mother. My friends' moms are basically okay. I mean, there's nothing actually *wrong* with any of them, but they do have their quirks. For example, Ellen's mother is incredibly limp and never seems to have any opinions. Margaret's mother has too *many* opinions and tends to freak out over everything, so we have to be really careful what we say in front of her. And Amy's mother is just the right balance, except that she works a ton and is hardly ever there, and it's mostly Rosalia—the house-keeper—who's in charge.

On the other hand, not one of those mothers ever wrote an article about the time her daughter, along with her friends, devised an elaborate and foolproof plan for get-ting into an R-rated movie, and how she (the mother) had to rush in at the last minute, like the Lone Ranger or somebody, and save us. The way mine did.

While I was sitting there pondering all that, Brian came into the kitchen, poured himself a bowl of cereal, and hacked a banana into blobs to go on top. He dumped milk over the whole thing and picked up the bowl, head-ing for the family room.

"Nuh-uh," I said, jumping up and moving around the table to intercept him. "No food in the family room. That's the rule." Actually, it's a rule in our house that gets broken about a million times over but it's still a rule. Be-sides, if Brian spilled that gloppy mess, I'd be stuck clean-ing it up. And Punch doesn't like bananas.

For a minute, Brian looked as if he was going to argue, but then he shrugged and let me take his bowl and put it on the table. I poured him some juice and tried not to listen to his slurping, slopping noises which pass for eating when nobody's there to correct him. Once he was done we headed into the family room to watch cartoons. Not that I *like* cartoons anymore—it's just that it's a Saturday-morning kind of thing to do. We were still sitting there when Mom came home.

"I can't believe the two of you are in front of the TV on a beautiful day like this," she said, clicking off the set.

My mother is a great one for projects, and I held my breath, waiting to see what she would come up with. It didn't take long.

"It's not a moment too soon to clean out the flower beds in back," she said. "I need to cut back the rosebushes and we can get to work on the weeds and dead leaves and sticks—get everything all clear so that if the good weather holds, your father can put the mulch down when he gets a chance. Now jump into some clothes and come outside. I bet we can get it done before lunch and still have time to do some errands before Brian's swimming."

Did I mention that my mother is one of those high-energy people? Especially in the morning. When everybody else is still stumbling around half asleep. Though she does seem to mellow as the day goes on.

"Hop!" she said as Brian and I sat on the couch still staring at the TV screen, as if expecting it to come back on. I got up and was slouching toward the hall when Brian bounced out of his chair and started bunny hopping across the floor, rattling windowpanes and pictures on the wall. It's one of many obnoxious things my brother does.

Once I was dressed and outside, Mom put me to work on the flower bed that runs along the fence between our house and Mrs. Batterton's. Mom started in on the rosebushes while Brian did not much of anything with a toothless rake down by the garage. The day wasn't what I'd actually call warm, and the ground felt cold and sort of clammy as I hacked at weeds and scooped leaves from around the fence posts. If you want my opinion, that fence, which is taller than I am, should be even taller. Like maybe up to the sky and with extra pickets where the spaces are now. That's on account of Mrs. Batterton (aka Mrs. Battle-ax) is the deluxe combo model of all the witches and ogres I've ever read about.

Last year my mom planted sunflowers along the fence because she said that way, when they grew tall, their heads would bobble over the fence and maybe cheer Mrs. Batterton some. She even wrote a column about how gardens are for sharing and should be designed with others in mind. As Mom's columns go, that was a pretty good one.

I was leaning on my rake thinking about how I'd actually cut that one out and saved it in my bottom drawer, when I heard the witch-woman's voice, practically in my ear.

"Charlotte, what are you doing over there?" she said.

"Not much, Mrs. Batterton," I said. "Just cleaning out the flower bed."

"Don't send any weeds my way. And I certainly hope your mother's not going to plant any of those ugly sunflowers this year. I felt as though they were watching me, every move I made." With that she made a humphing, sniffing noise and I watched through the pickets as she turned and walked away, her rubber galoshes flapping as she went.

I remembered my father had said that morning that I should have a talk with my mother, but somehow this didn't seem to be the time or place. Actually, all I felt like asking right then was—if *she* was into gardening, why did *I* get stuck doing it? And that, in turn, would lead to a lecture from Mom about the greater good of the family and how we *all* got to enjoy the garden, so we should all *help*. It might even lead to a column—one about teaching life's lessons over the flower bed. Yuck.

I didn't talk to my mother at Brian's swim practice either, mainly because Margaret was there and the two of us headed for the top row of the bleachers. We had a lot to talk about, especially the twin boys who had come with their parents to look at the house that was for sale next door to her. And what we would do if they ended up in our school, in our class. Besides, swim practice is pretty wild, with kids yelling and whistles blowing and everything sounding muffled and sort of steamy, the way they do at an indoor pool.

When we got home, late in the afternoon, Mom headed up to her study. "I've got a couple of hours of work to do," she said over her shoulder. "And I positively don't want to be disturbed. No matter what."

"But what if a tree falls on the house?" said Brian.

"It won't," my mother said.

"But what if it does? Or a rocket, or a spaceship?" Brian went on.

Mom turned when she got to the top of the steps and looked down at us. "If a tree falls on the house, Brian, or even a rocket or a spaceship, you be sure and tell me about it—*after* I've finished my work. Now give me this time, and when your father gets home and I've done what I have to do, we'll all go out to dinner. And you kids can pick the place. Okay?"

Brian shrugged and headed for the computer and one of those games he's always playing. I settled down to my homework.

I had just finished my math and was actively engaged in staring at the kitchen ceiling while I tried to decide what to do next, when the doorbell rang. Punch took off, tearing through the dining room, skidding across the hall floor, and scrunching up the rug, before he pounced at the sidelight next to the front door, barking at the glass. He was in full mailman alert.

Only it wasn't the mailman.

I took hold of Punch's collar and pulled him back while I opened the door, staring at the stranger who wasn't quite a stranger standing on the other side of the storm door. I was sure I'd never seen him before, but even so the floor seemed to tilt beneath me and there was a prickly feeling down the back of my neck.

"I'm here to see Dr. Flannigan," he said.

"He's not home," I said, shaking my head.

"How about Mrs. Flannigan, then. Is she in?"

And in spite of all the things Mom had said about not disturbing her, I nodded and said, "Yeah, wait a minute." Then I closed the door and walked upstairs and, without even knocking, opened the door to my mother's study.

"Mom, there's a kid—a guy—and he needs to see you now," I said.

"Tottie, what did I tell you? Remember? Not a tree or a

rocket or a spaceship. I've got to finish this article I'm working on. Now just tell whoever it is—"

"No, you've got to come. You've *got* to."

Mom sighed. She got up and followed me down the steps. She opened the door and then, after what seemed like a very long time with none of us saying anything, she unlocked the storm door and said, "Yes, I think you'd better come inside."

And with that, my mother led the stranger who was not quite a stranger into our house.

Zachary

"There's an earlier bus, you know," said the guy behind the counter, holding off punching whatever keys needed punching in order to make the machine spit out a ticket. "The five o'clock'll get you into Baltimore at—"

"That's okay," I said. "The one leaving at midnight'll do fine."

"Want to hang around and enjoy the hospitality awhile, huh?" he said, nodding at the scuzzy waiting room in back of me. "Well, be my guest. You want one-way or round-trip?"

The question pulled me up short. One-way or round-trip? It was a basic no-brainer, but when it came to answering, I froze. *One-way*, of course. But saying it out loud would be the same as saying I was never coming back. That I had no one to come back *to*.

"C'mon, fella, one-way or round-trip?" He sighed and looked up at the clock, as if to let me know I'd already used more than my allotted Greyhound moment.

"Sorry. One ticket, one-way." I handed over the money and tucked the ticket into my wallet between my library card and my school ID.

After that meaningful exchange, I retrieved a three-day-old newspaper from the top of a trash can, found a seat, and settled down to read. We're not exactly talking current events here, but hey, I'd been out of touch for so long it was all news to me. Anyway, it kept me occupied, at least until the realization set in that bus stations could cause mind rot, or brain fungus. Or worse. There was something about the atmosphere that seemed to deaden the senses.

I watched people slouching or sleeping or just staring into space, and then, more to wake myself up than anything else, I grabbed my backpack and headed for the door. I stood outside studying a panhandler and listening as he changed his spiel from one person to the next. He had to get to Cleveland, to Texas, to Montreal; he had a sick kid, a dying aunt, a job waiting in another city. When he began to repeat himself, I took off in search of a McDonald's.

After refueling with a Big Mac and fries, I found a newsstand and bought the thickest paperback I could get, going strictly for quantity, not quality. By then it was three o'clock—nine hours till departure time. I could've gone back, found my buddy behind the ticket counter, told him he was right all along, and asked for a trade-in to that earlier bus. I could've, but I *couldn't*. For some wacko reason I didn't begin to understand, I was determined to hang in there until midnight. The witching hour.

I set out, then, walking the streets, breathing exhaust fumes and thinking non-thoughts, such as whether there is some kind of zoning law that says all streets surrounding a bus station have to have the same grungy look.

Back in the waiting room, a whole new cast of characters were in place. I checked them out long enough to see they had their parts down pat: they slept and slouched and stared into space like pros. With that taken care of, I got out my book, sliding down into a bus-station slump and trying to catch the story line. But as I read, there seemed to be words running along the bottom of the page, like sometimes happens with TV news, that reached out and grabbed at me.

You could call Tony, or Pete, or Scott—there's a pay phone right over there and—

And what? Say goodbye, so long, it's been a blast?

Tony's mom's okay. She'd let you hang for a while—

Till when—I graduate from high school? And what—
feed me and clothe me along the way? Get real.

*Go back to the apartment, then. Sell what's there, it's
yours anyway. You can make it on your own. People do.*

Yeah, sure. How long d'you think it'd be before the Social Services people would be on my tail? They're probably still there, waiting for me to turn up, ready with the
whole *Oliver Twist* routine. Or maybe the panhandler out
front'd let me squat on his territory. No thanks.

I slammed my book closed and shoved it down inside
my backpack. I opened the outside pocket to make sure
my mother's letter was still there, then went to find a
Coke.

The bus left just past midnight. By then I was so totally
beat I figured I'd sleep the whole way, but it didn't happen. The old guy next to me snored like a band saw, but
even if he'd been singing lullabies, I'd have been awake.
No sooner had we pulled away from the platform than
the avalanche of memories I'd been holding at bay came
crashing down around me.

They were all there. Equal-opportunity thoughts. Mom's
illness and the talks we'd had, especially toward the end.
The hospice people and how they'd been there for us, how
Sara and some other friends said all that great stuff at the

funeral, and what it was like when I made myself go back to school. And came home afterward to an empty place.

My mother was dead and was never coming back. I had made a promise to her and now I was being propelled through the dark to keep that promise to go to a father I didn't know and didn't want to know.

I was alone and all I really wanted was to kick the crap out of someone or something.

We made a rest stop at about four in the morning, and I crawled over the band-saw guy and got out to grab a cup of coffee. I could stay here, I thought. Let the bus go on without me and start a new life in Somewhere, USA. But when the driver blew his horn, I hurried back and settled into my seat as if I belonged there. It's an interesting idea—a bus as a security blanket.

Once we were under way again, the thoughts came crowding back. I fought them off as best I could until dawn, and after that I concentrated on staring through the grimy windowpane all the rest of the way to Baltimore.

Based on a survey of two, bus stations are all alike. I cleaned up in the men's room, keeping a weirdo watch and hanging on to my backpack. After that I ate a burger at a lunch counter and washed it down with grape soda. I checked the address in the phone book to make sure it was the one Mom had given me, and then I sat on a bench watching the schedule board and wondering what I was doing there.

I walked around outside and came back to the waiting room and read three chapters of my book. It wasn't until late afternoon that I worked up the nerve to ask the lady at the information window how to get where I needed to go.

"Outside and to the left for a couple of blocks," she said. "That's where you catch the number-ten bus."

I said thanks and headed for the door. My teeth were scummy and my head felt numb from too little sleep and not enough real food. And the way I figured it, I was about to give someone a hell of a shock.

Tottie

"I just want you to know that I'm not here to make trouble for anybody," the boy said. "It's just that—just—"

"You're hungry, aren't you?" my mother asked, totally ignoring what he was trying to say. "Come on into the kitchen and I'll get you something. We can talk later. When my husband gets home."

I followed the two of them, settling myself on a stool by the breakfast bar and trying to blend into the background, hoping Mom wouldn't notice and tell me to go find something else to do. I needn't have bothered, though, because my mother had her head in the refrigerator and was pulling out packages and jars and bottles.

"I have ham and turkey and Swiss cheese. Rye bread

and wheat. Now you'll have to tell me if you like mayonnaise, and how about mustard—there's Dijon and just regular and I think there's something really spicy in the cupboard. Pickles? There's dill, and maybe some gherkins. And what about to drink? Milk? Soda? Would you rather have something hot?" It seemed as if Mom was going to work her way through the entire contents of the fridge and then go on to the cupboards.

The stranger held up his hand and said, "Anything's fine with me. Really."

He sat there at the kitchen table looking at my mother as she piled meat and cheese and pickle slices onto bread and then added mayo *and* mustard. And the whole time he was watching her, I was watching him. He was sixteen, or maybe seventeen, tall, and I guess what you'd call lanky. He had hair that was red like a flame, a ton of freckles, and a big nose. The same quivery feeling I'd had when I first saw him came back. The back of my neck prickled again.

"Who *are* you?" I said, the words popping out before I could decide if I really wanted to know.

"My name is Zachary Pearce. Zach for short," he said.

"Oh, I'm sorry . . . I should've . . . I mean, this is my daughter, Tottie, and her brother, Brian, is around here somewhere. And I'm Winnie—Winnie Flannigan." Mom wiped her hand on the side of her jeans and held it out for him to shake. "Now let me get you some milk," she went on. "We have one percent or skim—whichever you want."

Zachary Pearce looked at her as if, up to now, he'd always just thought that milk was milk.

"Take one percent," I said. "The skim is blue and gross."

"Tottie, maybe you'd better run along and finish what you were doing," my mother said in that zap-and-you're-gone way parents sometimes use when they want kids to disappear.

"This *is* what I was doing." I pointed to my books spread over one end of the table.

"Oh," said Mom, as if that settled that. And I guess in a way it did because she took out a glass and poured the milk, and I went back to trying to fade into the woodwork.

She put the milk and a plate of sandwiches on the table in front of Zachary. "If you want anything else, let me know," she said.

Then Mom and I watched the stranger eat. We heard the pickles crunch and the glunking noise as he took the first swallow of milk. That's when I decided that no matter who he was, we shouldn't stare at him like maybe it was feeding time at the zoo. I grabbed a bag of pretzels off the top of the fridge, deliberately rustling the plastic as I unrolled the top and reached inside. With that, Brian and Punch raced into the kitchen and stood next to me.

"I want some," said Brian, and I handed him a pretzel and dropped one on the floor for the dog. My brother stuffed his into his mouth and turned to look at Zachary for the first time. "Who are you?" he said. "You look like someone."

He's a cousin, I wanted to say, but didn't. *That's who he is—some distant cousin we never knew we had.*

My mother turned away and went to stand by the window. The prickly feeling on my neck turned to electric shocks as I reached into the bag again, grabbing a handful of pretzels and shoving them at Brian. "Here, take these with you. Back to whatever you were doing. Now go on and go."

After Brian left, with Punch close behind, the giant silence settled back over the kitchen. Finally, when I couldn't stand it anymore, I rattled the pretzel bag again, opening and closing it. Opening and closing. Zachary picked up another sandwich and bit into it. Mom turned the water on, then off.

"Where have you been living all these years?" she said, turning around.

"In Ohio—Cincinnati," said Zachary.

"That's where your family is?"

Zachary shook his head as if he didn't understand Mom's question. "There's never been much in the way of family except for my mother," he said. "Well, there was my grandmother, but she died when I was nine, and since then it's just been Mom and me. And some cousins in Texas I've never met."

"But your adoptive family? A mother and a father? Do they know you're here?"

"There was always just my mom, and she died a week and a half ago." He picked up half of a sandwich and held it, without actually biting into it.

"I'm so sorry," my mother said. "I really am. I—you—I guess this really will have to wait until my husband gets home. He won't be much longer."

The whole time they were talking, I kept looking from one to the other, trying to make sense of what they were saying. It was weird because, even though they were speaking English, it was as if their words were coming out in a different language.

Then Mom got busy putting away the ham and turkey and cheese, the mustard and mayo, and the two kinds of pickles. Zachary went back to eating, and I watched the clock on the stove as it clicked the minutes away.

As soon as we heard Dad's car on the driveway, my mother hurried out to meet him. For a minute I could see them through the window, until they moved out of sight. Then it was just Zachary and me. And that killer silence.

"How'd you get here?" I finally asked.

"On the bus," he said.

"No, I mean from Ohio. How'd you get *here*—to Baltimore?"

"On the bus," he said again.

"Without any stuff? Not even a toothbrush?"

"I have a backpack, but I left it at the bus station."

"How old are you?"

"Seventeen. How about you?"

"I'm thirteen. And Brian's seven."

That about did it for conversation. Zachary took his plate and glass to the sink and washed and dried them, setting them on the counter. I went back to watching the clock, as if it were the most amazing thing I'd ever seen. And at 4:53 p.m. Dad came in the back door.

As he walked across the kitchen, his forehead crinkled the way it does when he has things on his mind. He held out his hand and said, "Zachary? I'm David Flannigan."

I watched the stranger's forehead crinkle in the exact same way, as he shook my father's hand.

Zachary

The house was right out of *Leave It to Beaver*. Any minute I expected to see Wally and the Beaver come out the front door, with Mr. and Mrs. Cleaver in hot pursuit. Then a rotten idea took hold: maybe I was supposed to be the Eddie Haskell in this whole thing. Maybe my job was to really lay it on thick, with a shovel. *Yes, Mrs. Cleaver. You're absolutely right, Mr. Cleaver. Anything I can do to help*. It made me gag.

I stood across the street, checking out the house, mentally trying to put my mother into the picture, the way Mrs. Brenner did with the three bears and that flannel board–thing she used in kindergarten. I stuck Mom on, halfway between the front door and the minivan in the driveway. Then I yanked her off again. No way was this her scene.

The thing about my mother is that she always had her own agenda. She was into her job as a paralegal, into getting through law school, and also into a bunch of causes like the Sierra Club and Citizens Against Handguns. She was anti-*things* too: refrigerators that spit out ice cubes automatically, giant-screen TVs, and name-brand clothes. The cool thing was, she never let backing out of the adoption she and my father had agreed on change who she was, or how she had planned her life.

If Mom was set on her own agenda, she was equally determined that I have mine, too. "We're not going to be one of those wussy mother-son combos," she drilled into me, back when other mothers were still reciting "Humpty Dumpty" to their kids. She pushed me into Cub Scouts, then pretended not to be disappointed when I dropped out. She sat through endless Little League games, always with a book on her lap, and tried hard to look up at all the right times. She nagged about the value of money and how I should get a job, but didn't freak out when I spent my first paycheck on a new pair of Nikes instead of wearing the cheapos she was willing to buy.

She talked independence, and at the same time she was the safety net stretched out underneath me. And when she got sick, that didn't change. Not in the beginning, anyway. Even when things got really bad, she'd manage to pull herself up and ask if I'd finished my social studies paper, or was eating right, or managing to keep ahead of the laundry—which in mother-speak meant changing my shirt for school every day.

Then she was gone, and so was the net. And I was on some frigging street in Baltimore thinking half-baked thoughts about ice cubes and clean shirts. I kicked at a lamppost and forced myself to move and next thing I knew, I was on the porch, ringing the bell.

The dog got there first, a spotted, slobbering beast, followed by a girl with a ponytail, who I guessed was twelve, maybe thirteen. She did one of those cartoon double-take things and told me to wait a minute. She disappeared and I was alone on the porch again, with the dog barking and clawing at the glass alongside the front door. It was *Leave It to Beaver* meets *101 Dalmatians*.

The girl came back, this time with a woman who went through the same I've-just-seen-a-ghost routine, and suddenly I was in the kitchen eating ham sandwiches. The woman, whose name was Winnie, was a total freak-out, talking nonstop about mustard or mayo, skim milk or plain. The girl, Tottie, watched, and there was a little kid who was in and then out again.

He came home at five o'clock. David Edward Flannigan, MD. Father. He shook my hand and my skin crawled and I felt sure I was looking in a mirror.

This isn't going to work, I thought. *Tomorrow I'm out of here.*

Tottie

There was no way we were going out to dinner *that* night. In fact, by the time the day was over, I was pretty sure I was never going to leave my house again.

The first thing that happened was that my father took Zachary into the den and closed the door. What I really wanted to do was to tiptoe after them—to press my ear up against the wood, to peer through the keyhole. (Except our doors don't have keyholes.) But with my mom standing there, wiping at the same place on the counter over and over, I knew better than to try it.

"Is he going to stay?" I asked.

"I don't know what's going to happen," my mother said.

"I don't see why he *should*. Stay here, I mean."

"I think you *do* see, Tottie." She scrubbed at the counter even harder.

"What if he's a crook, or an ax murderer? What about how you always said not to let strangers into the house?"

"Zachary may be a stranger to us now but—"

"What do we actually *know* about him?" I broke in. "Maybe he just got our name out of the telephone book. What then?"

"I'm sure that's some of what your father's trying to determine now." Scrub, scrub, scrub.

"Why do you want him here?"

"I don't know if I do," my mother said. "To be totally honest, I don't know if I do. I guess all I can say is that I want what I want to be the right thing for all of us."

What *I* wanted was to keep throwing questions at her like darts at a board. I wanted them to sting, or maybe even hurt her, because she was the one who was here, while my father was out of reach, behind a shut-tight door with a perfect stranger. But before I could think of what to say next, the telephone rang. Mom answered and held it out to me. "Margaret," she mouthed.

"Hi," said Margaret. "You want to come over? My parents are going out but my mom said to tell your mom they'll be right next door. Anyway, Amy's coming and

Ellen if she gets home from her grandmother's in time. We can get a movie and—"

"I can't," I said.

"How come? You said before you weren't doing anything."

"I just can't, is all."

"You sound funny, choky, sort of," Margaret said. "Is anything wrong?"

"It's just allergies," I said.

"You don't have allergies."

"I do now," I said. "Anyway, I'll see you."

"Yeah, okay. See you," said Margaret, and we both hung up at the same time.

Just a minute later the phone rang again, and before I got a chance to reach for it, Brian appeared at my elbow. It's a really spooky thing about my brother—the way he knows the phone is for him before anyone even has a chance to answer it. I said "Hello," just to make sure, but as soon as I heard Teddy's voice I handed the receiver to Brian.

"Yeah. Right. See ya," he said into the phone. Then to Mom he added, "I'm going to Teddy's. Okay?"

"That's fine, but remember, when the Burtons are ready to eat dinner you come on home." My mother ran her fingers over the invisible spot on the counter and picked up the sponge again.

I was all set to fire more word darts at her, but just then my father opened the door to the den and called, "Winnie, can you come in here, please."

I followed Mom down the hall, but when we got to the door Dad put out his hand and caught me by the arm. "I need to talk to your mother privately for a few minutes, Tottie," he said.

"*He's* in there," I said, jerking my head toward Zachary, who was standing by the window. "Besides, I'm a member of this family."

"Let her come in, Dave," said Mom. My father nodded and stood back as the two of us went in and sat on the couch. He motioned Zachary to the rocker and settled himself into the slouchy green leather chair where he usually sat.

"Well," he said, steepling his fingers and leaning forward. "I guess the best thing to do is start at the beginning. This is Zachary Pearce, and as your mother knows, Tottie, and I guess you've figured out, he is my son."

I couldn't breathe. I put my hands up to my throat to fight off whatever was choking me, but I still couldn't breathe. I tried to cry out, to speak, to gasp, but nothing happened.

"*Tottie.*" My father's voice was quick and sharp, like a smack. "Tottie, are you with me?" he said.

"I hear you." My words seemed to trail along hours after his question. I looked down at the holes in the knees of my jeans, studying them as if they were important, and inched closer to my mother. "But why *is* he?" I said in a scrunched-up voice.

"Why is Zachary my son?" my father asked. Then he sighed. "Because a long time ago, when I was barely out of medical school and was still a resident at a hospital in New York, I met a young woman named Susan Pearce."

I wouldn't look at his face, but I watched as he locked his hands and bent his fingers back so that the knuckles cracked. "One night," he went on, "we did something very foolish."

I shook my head to keep him from telling me what he and Susan Pearce had done. I mean I *knew*, but I didn't *want* to know. Not about my *father*.

He kept on talking, his words coming slowly and carefully, as if he wanted to make sure I heard it all. "Some time later, when we weren't even seeing each other anymore, she called to tell me she was pregnant," my father said. "We got together for coffee the next day and talked about it and . . . well, the thing was, this wasn't a relationship in any sense of the word except maybe . . ." He tortured his fingers some more, the whole time staring down at the rug, and then went on. "We'd met at a party.

There was some alcohol involved, and I guess I'd have to say we weren't thinking right. I was in the middle of my residency and—"

"You've said that, Dave," my mother said.

Dad nodded. "And Susan Pearce was in her second year of law school and, as I recall, terribly ambitious."

He called her *Susan Pearce* again, like maybe he didn't know her well enough to just call her Susan.

"Anyway, we got together over coffee and talked for a long time. We finally decided, I mean neither one of us believed in abortion, that she would go back home to Cincinnati and have the baby and then give it up for adoption. I gave her money for medical expenses and a letter saying I was willing for the child to be adopted. There are so many couples desperate for children and—"

"That was her cover story," interrupted Zachary. "She went back to Ohio because she knew, well, between her and the guy there wasn't anything. Only then when she had the kid—me—she didn't go through with it. And she never got to finish law school."

My father cleared his throat and looked first at my mother and then at me. "I just found out this afternoon that all this time Zachary has been living with his mother, until she died a week and a half ago. She made him promise that he would come to me, when the time came, and even put it all in a letter, with instructions on how to get in touch. Susan Pearce worked as a paralegal, but her last illness was expensive and . . ." He stopped and shook his head, turning to Zachary. "I've always been so sure that you had been adopted by a good family."

"And conveniently you never thought of it again. Right? Never thought of my mother *or* her kid?" Zachary's voice lashed out.

"You don't know what you're talking about." My father brought his hand down hard on the arm of his chair. He leaned toward Zachary, as if they were the only two in the room. "Your mother and I had an agreement, and I had no reason to think she hadn't honored it. That she hadn't gone ahead with her life and her plans. And as for you—I've kept mental track of you all these years, watching the children your age I saw in the office and wondering if they were anything like you."

I slid my hand over on the couch and my mother covered it with hers. Just hearing about my father's secret life and thoughts made my skin crawl.

"Did Mom know?" I asked.

"Yes, she did, Tottie. When we first talked about getting married, I told her. But like me, your mother has always assumed that Zachary was adopted. Only, of course, we didn't know him as Zachary then."

After that, nobody said anything for a while. The phone rang and we let the machine get it. The clock in the front hall struck six.

"Look," said Zachary, twisting his fingers back the way my father had twisted his own. "I said before, I'm not here to make any trouble. I don't even have to stay, it's just that I promised my mom I'd get in touch, and then when I found out that Mr. Reynolds had called Social Services—"

My father held his hand up to stop him. "You did the right thing. My wife and I had a chance to talk a bit on the driveway when I first got home, and we'll talk more later, but meanwhile we—"

"Wait, Dave," my mother said. She stopped and looked from my father to the boy before she went on. "Zach, we'd like for you to stay."

I wanted to call her a traitor, but before I could catch my breath, I heard my father say, "Tottie?"

I shaped *no*'s and *never*'s inside my head, but my mother squeezed my fingers till they hurt, and I swallowed hard and said, "Yeah. Whatever."

"Well, good, good. That's settled then." Dad sat back with a look of relief creeping across his face as though he'd just figured out how to solve the problem of global warming or something.

Right. Sure, Dad, I wanted to shout. *That's it? You've just ruined our lives and you think things are settled?*

Before we had a chance to say anything else, there was a *clatter-bang-crash* at the back door. It continued on down the hall and into the room as Brian appeared, trailing ropes with tin cans on the ends. "Me and Teddy made stilts," he said. "Is it time to go to dinner yet?"

"Dinner?" said Dad.

"I promised Tottie and Brian we'd all go out to dinner," Mom said. "But that was earlier. Before—"

"Hey, you're still here," said Brian, balancing himself on his can-stilts and turning to face Zachary. "Are you going to dinner, too?"

The words flew out of my mouth before I had a chance to catch them. "If we go, *he's* going, too, because he's your *brother*."

Brian clumped closer to Zachary, as if to see him better. "A real brother? That's cool, on account of now there're two of us and just one of Tottie."

My mother jumped up. "I think that instead of going out, we'll just call for pizza. We usually get one pepperoni and one veggie. Is that okay with you, Zachary?"

Mom hardly waited for him to nod before she went on. "I'll make a salad, and Tottie, you phone in the order.

Brian, take those things off in the house. And I think your father wants to talk to you."

When the man in the pizza place answered the phone and asked for my order, I didn't know what to say. I mean we—our regular family—ate two mediums. But now our family was suddenly lopsided.

Zachary

I really screwed things up by coming here. I knew, when I was standing on the other side of the street checking out *Leave It to Beaver*–ville, that this wasn't my scene. I knew it again as I sat in the kitchen chowing down on turkey-and-ham sandwiches. But before I could get it together enough to even think about bolting, he was home and we were into some heart-to-heart.

Reality check here. There were plenty of times, when I was younger, that I wanted him to walk into my life. There were times when I bugged my mother about why we couldn't see him. *Other kids*, I taunted her, *see their dads. Other kids go for visits. Or to the zoo. To Disney World. With their dads.*

Eventually, her answers came automatically. "This is who we are, Zach. And this is the way we're going to do it. On our own, without help from anyone."

There were times, too, when I was playing Little League and I'd look up into the stands, sure that he was there. The guy with the Yankees cap, maybe, or even the dude in the wheelchair who showed up for almost every game the year I was in seventh grade, and always disappeared just before the last inning.

Other times I knew he was on a life-threatening mission. Maybe he was a double agent somewhere and it was the CIA that kept him from getting in touch. Or else he was an astronaut, locked into an incredible endless orbit that NASA wasn't letting on about.

Now my mother was gone and he was here, or I was there, and I didn't want any part of him.

"I'm sorry about your mother," my father said. "That must have been hard for you."

I shrugged. No way I was going to lose my cool in front of him. Besides, all I wanted, right then, was to bait him. "She said you weren't simpatico. That there wasn't any spark between you."

"We were young is what we were," he said.

"Not all that young."

"And not all that prepared for the consequences."

"That would be me?" I couldn't resist.

"No, no, I didn't mean—"

"But I *was* the consequence, right?" I said.

He arranged his face into a you-can't-rile-me expression, and I suddenly knew how he must look doling out injections to kids who didn't want to get them. "You know, I think I always knew there was a chance that once you were older, and with your adoptive parents' blessings, you might come looking for your birth mother and father. I thought—"

"She said she wasn't keen on the whole adoption idea—my mother, I mean—but decided to go along up until the time . . . till when . . ."

"Until she saw you, right?" he said, and when I nodded he went on. "I'm glad Susan did what she did. I'm glad you had her all these years, but I'm only sorry I didn't know so we could have worked something out before this, made some arrangements."

"She didn't want your money. Said we were going to make it on our own. And we were doing fine up until—"

I stopped, and he didn't pick up the slack. We sat for a while, listening to the clock, and then I reached into my pocket and took out my mother's letter. I dug my birth certificate out of my wallet, along with my school ID, my library card, my Blockbuster card, and handed them to him. "I guess you ought to look at these, just so you'll know I'm who I say I am."

He read the letter through quickly and then went back and reread it. I watched him run his finger over the seal on the birth certificate, waiting to see what he'd say when he saw the words *David Edward Flannigan* in the space next to FATHER'S NAME. He checked out the cards and handed them all back to me. "You know, Zachary, this is all well and good," he said, "but just looking at you tells me all I really need to know."

I put my hand up to my face, then pulled it away. I felt tired and weighted down, as if I were carrying some stranger on my back.

That quick he shifted gears on me and was into over-drive—Tarzan to the rescue. "I'm sure there are things to be taken care of, on the other end," he said, getting up and going to his desk for a pencil and a yellow pad. "Is there anyone back in Ohio I can contact? Anyone who was in charge of Susan's affairs?"

"One of the lawyers in the firm where she worked, I guess. He's the one who wrote her will and then after-ward, when the firm said they'd take care of the funeral and all, he made the arrangements."

"Good," he said, handing me the paper. "If you give me his name and the name of the firm, I'll get in touch. Now, you and your mother had a—what—a house? An apartment?"

"An apartment. On East Walnut."

"There have to be things—belongings—that you left behind."

That's when it struck me for the first time—that I actually had walked off and left it all there. The chairs and beds and tables we'd always lived with. Mom's books, the TV, my stereo, and even my Walkman.

He was still going on, pushing at me. "Write down what you want and we'll have it sent. There're people who take care of things like that. We'll need to contact the school, for your records. And as for the things in the apartment you don't want, we'll authorize that they be sold. If that's okay with you."

My life was being ripped out from under me, and he was asking if it was okay. This must've shown on my face, because all of a sudden he made a U-turn. "Don't worry about that right now," he said. "Sometime in the next few days."

The clock kept ticking and we kept listening. I thought we were about to move into some heavy father-son kind of thing, but after a while he stood up, headed for the door, and said, "I'm going to ask Winnie to come in now, and we'll talk some more."

Winnie came, with Tottie trailing behind her, and we were into this great public-forum thing. The Cleavers meet Mystery Man. All we needed was the kid, Brian, and maybe some neighbors, and a bunch of relatives.

I pulled myself up short. I wasn't the Mystery Man. I knew exactly who I was. Zachary Alan Pearce. *ZAP*. I was a baseball player, and sometimes a runner. A sort of history buff who liked natural-disaster movies—avalanches and earthquakes and volcanoes, that kind of thing. I hung out with Tony and Pete and Scott, with Josh and Ezra, and was halfway thinking of asking Jessica Finan to my junior prom. I was really into the Dead, the Who, and even some of my mom's Bob Dylan stuff, though the one time she took me to the symphony I counted every tile in the ceiling before it was over. But I was only nine at the time.

Somewhere in back of all these thoughts about who I was, I heard the doctor telling them what they already knew—that I was his *son*. He said it out loud, and sort of deadpan, letting the word hang there in the room. Winnie's face was smooth, and blank, revealing nothing. Tottie looked as if she was about to puke.

He told the story, and it was totally weird to hear him talk about my mother as if she were some person he didn't know. Susan Pearce this and Susan Pearce that. He talked about the adoption that wasn't and then smooth-talked his way into saying how I'd done the right thing in coming here. But the whole time he seemed ready to blow his top—a disaster movie in the making.

And after all that, it was Winnie who asked me to stay.

Somewhere along the way, Brian came in and I heard Tottie say, ". . . he's your brother" in the kind of voice she would've used to say, "He's got anthrax."

Brian said, "Cool," right off, without stopping to think. Which was okay, I guess, except that I wanted to be back in Cincinnati. I wanted to be around people who really knew me, who knew my mom. People from school, or work, or down the street, or even from that book club she belonged to that sometimes met at our apartment.

Tottie

I ended up ordering an extra-large veggie pizza and a medium pepperoni one, and when we had finished supper there was still a ton left over. Mostly because Brian was the only one actually eating. Zachary had this I'll-get-it-down-no-matter-what look, and the rest of us just picked. Dad folded and unfolded the same piece of pepperoni pizza till it was worn and tired-looking. Mom pushed a slice of veggie pizza around her plate and didn't even yell at me when I rolled bits of cheese into pellets and piled them up like miniature cannonballs.

After we ate, or didn't eat, Dad and Brian took Zachary down to the bus station to pick up his backpack. What I can't figure out is why he didn't bring it with him in the first place—unless he was planning to just check us out. Which gave me a glimmer of hope that he might actually hop another bus and disappear. Talk about kidding myself!

As soon as they'd gone, Mom and I headed upstairs to get a room ready. The minute we got to the third floor, I was on the attack.

"That was a hideously traitory thing to do," I said. "Why did you?"

"Why did I what?" my mother said as she peeled off the bedspread and started to fit a blue plaid sheet over the mattress.

"You know what. Why'd you ask him to stay? Why'd you say you *wanted* him to stay when before, in the kitchen, you said you didn't *know* what you wanted?"

"I also said that I wanted what I wanted to be the best thing for all of us, and I somehow think this will be." Mom shook out the top sheet so that it cracked like a whip before drifting down onto the bed.

"It's not the best thing for me," I said. "And it never will be—not in a zillion years. So why did you?"

"Did you see his face?" she asked.

"You mean did I see his face and how it looks like Dad's? Well, yeah, sort of, except you know what? I bet he did that on purpose. I bet he frizzed his hair and dyed it red so's we'd take him in and then he could hold us hostage and steal our money and everything. You read about that kind of thing happening all the time."

Mom tucked in the covers and put the spread back on the bed, as if I hadn't said any of that big mouthful. "Did you see his face, the way it looked when your father was telling us his story? Did you?"

"I guess, but still I don't see why . . ." I sat on the edge of the bed and my mother stood across from me, stuffing a pillow into a sham.

"He's seventeen years old and his mother just died, Tottie," my mother said, speaking slowly and carefully. "Whatever money there was is gone, and now he's on his own."

"Lots of people are," I said, feeling meanness prickle all over me.

"What if *you* were in his situation? Or Brian?"

"Well, there has to be somebody. People he knows. Friends of his mother. Anyway, he's got cousins in Texas. He said so."

"Cousins he's never met."

"He could meet them," I said. "You guys could put him on a plane for Texas and he could *meet* them."

"But his father is here." My mother's voice, though soft

and low, was somehow louder than anything I'd ever heard.

His father is here. The words echoed in my head. *His father is here.* Only he's my father, too.

"Why didn't he marry her then—that Susan person?" The words shot out before I had a chance to think, but then, all in a rush, my thoughts caught up to my mouth. If my father had married Susan Pearce, then he wouldn't have married my mother and then I wouldn't exist. Or Brian either. We wouldn't live in this house or have Punch or Erlich or any of our friends. And if my mom wrote her newspaper column, she wouldn't be named Winnie *Flannigan* and she'd be writing about some totally different family.

I shivered and picked up a pillow to try and warm myself. As if she knew what I had been thinking, Mom sat beside me and put her arm around my shoulder. "We can't change what's happened—all we can do is go on," she said.

"How?"

"By doing the best we can." I could have guessed, before she even said it, that that was what my mother was going to say on account of that's what she *always* says. No matter what. *Just do the best you can . . . the best you can . . . the best you can . . .*

"And," she continued, "by trying to see this from

Zachary's point of view. Now how about running downstairs and getting some towels for this bathroom, while I make sure there's nothing in the bureau drawers."

I got the towels and hung them in the bathroom, then stood in the doorway looking into the room. It was warm and cozy, with its slanty ceilings and bright blue rug and a heap of throw pillows piled on the beds. And suddenly, I wanted it. "I always thought I'd get this room," I said, watching the way the lamp made a pool of light on the desk. "That I would move up here and have total privacy and then when one of my friends slept over you wouldn't hear us and be all the time telling us to be quiet. I thought—"

"You don't even *like* the third floor," said Mom, rolling her eyes. "Remember last year when your room was being painted and we wanted you to sleep here for a couple of days? You ended up coming down to the guest room."

"You could have put *him* in the guest room," I said.

"He's not company . . . he's . . . I guess . . . one of us. Anyway, Nanny and Granddad are coming next week and I'll need that room for them." Mom stopped, as if she were suddenly out of breath. She ran her fingers through her hair and reached out to catch hold of the dresser.

I felt a sort of smirk creep across my face as I turned and went downstairs, leaving my mother to figure out how she was going to break the news to *her* mother and father about this new member of the family.

In our family we go to church every Sunday. Even on vacation. Except when we're a million miles from anywhere, and that doesn't happen very often. Regular Sundays, though, we go to the nine o'clock mass at Saints Philip and James, where for just that service the organist plays a piano and somebody else plays a guitar and there are a bunch of really cool hymns. And where my father sings louder than anybody else. Dad has a good voice and all, but as soon as he opens his mouth I sort of slither to the far end of the pew and hope people will think I'm not with him. That's because I'm convinced that everybody in the entire church can hear him. Which may be true, because lots of times, when mass is over, perfect strangers come up and tell him how much they like his voice. As far as I'm concerned, that just encourages him to sing louder the next week.

Anyway, the day after Zachary showed up at our house was a Sunday, and once Dad had awakened Brian and me, I heard him heading up to the third floor to rouse Zachary out of bed. I don't know whether he gave him a choice or not, but at a quarter to nine Zachary was standing in the kitchen, ready to go. He had on the same paint-splattered jeans he'd worn the day before and a wrinkled blue shirt with sleeves that didn't come even close to his wrists. One thing I like about our church is that you don't have to be dressed up to go there, but even so I could see my mother biting on her lip to keep from saying that maybe that was pushing casual to the outer limits. Which is what she would have said to Brian or me.

Something really weird happened when we got to church. We went in the same as usual and sat where we always sit, up front and to the side. Dad picked up his hymnal and opened it the same as usual. But he didn't sing. Not the entrance hymn, or the "Gloria," or anything along the way. Not even "The Hymn to Joy" at the very end, which I happen to know is one of his favorites. And then, when mass was over, instead of standing around outside and talking, he hustled us across the street and into the car, not even stopping for bagels on the way home.

The way I figure it, we should have stopped for bagels, because if we had, we might have missed Mrs. Batterton, who was out walking her dog, Toby. Toby is an incredibly ugly dog with a smooshed-in face and a snuffly nose, and just as we pulled into the driveway he was taking a tremendous dump right on our front lawn.

"Bet she won't clean it up—she never does," I mumbled, but wonder of wonders, there was Mrs. Batterton fishing a yellow plastic newspaper bag out of her pocket and leaning over to pick up the poop. She straightened, tied a knot in the end of the bag, and stood watching as we all got out of the car. Mom. Me. Brian. Dad. And Zachary.

The minute she saw Zachary she started toward us, tugging on Toby's leash and pulling him along the driveway. "Family visiting?" she called. "I saw the young man out front yesterday and I said to myself he must be kin to Dr. Flannigan. What with that hair—that strong family likeness. Is he here for long?"

All of a sudden, as if he were a Border collie on patrol, my father was herding us all toward the back door. When we were partway there, he seemed to change his mind, though, and swung around to face Mrs. Batterton. "This is my son," he said. "And his name is Zachary."

We'd no sooner gotten into our house from church than the rain started. It was a soppy, cold, settling-in rain that made me just know the whole world was crying because Zachary Pearce had come to live at our house. I tried that in a poem I wrote for school this year—having the sky weep on account of something really sad—and Mr. Zimmerman, my English teacher, said it was a *pathetic fallacy* and not to do it. Things were definitely pathetic at our house and if you ask me, the world *was* crying.

Take breakfast, for example. All of a sudden we didn't fit at our cozy kitchen table and had to eat in the dining room. With a tablecloth and all, the way we do when we have company. Even though my mother had said, just the night before, that Zachary wasn't company. Once we were there, around the table with *The Baltimore Sun* and *The New York Times* spread out in front of us, nobody said anything. It wasn't one of those comfortable breakfast silences with everybody crunching cereal and rattling newspapers. It was just a stretching-out kind of quiet that continued on through the rest of the morning and lunch and into the afternoon. For once, even Brian didn't blather on.

My mother and father had a couple of whispered conversations in hallways and corners, and my father spent some time on the phone. Along about mid-afternoon he came into the family room, where the rest of us were not exactly watching an old movie on TV. "Well, Zachary," he said, "let's head out to the mall and get you a few things—you know, jeans and shirts—so you'll have them to start school. Anybody else want to go?"

"I do," said Brian, who seemed to have gobbled up this big brother business.

"How about you, Tottie?"

"No, thanks," I said, scrunching down lower on the couch and staring at the TV as though I really cared what was on the screen.

The sky kept crying or the rain kept raining all afternoon. The movie ended and another one started up without my mother even saying to turn that thing off. About four-thirty Amy showed up, and Mom sent her into the family room.

"What're you watching?" she said, settling onto the couch beside me.

"I don't know. Some old movie with Fred Astaire and a lot of dancing."

Maybe some terrible virus had taken over our house, because now Amy and I had nothing to say to each other either. We just kept sitting there watching Fred and some woman twirl and leap and swoop and spin till I guess Amy figured it was as boring at my house as it was at hers and got ready to leave.

I dragged myself up off the couch to walk her to the door, and we got to the kitchen just in time to see Dad, Brian, and Zachary come in and head for the hall closet.

"Who was that?" said Amy as I followed her onto the back steps.

"Just somebody," I said.

"Somebody who?"

"His name is Zachary."

"Who's Zachary?"

"Some kid who's staying here," I said.

"What kind of kid?" said Amy. "He looks like your dad."

"He was sopping wet—how can you tell what he looked like?" I asked.

"I just could. He looks more like your dad than even you and Brian."

"That's because he's his father," I said. "My father is *his* father, I mean."

"But I never knew your dad had been married before." Amy pulled up her hood and looked at me as if I were suddenly speaking Chinese.

"He wasn't," I said. Then I knew there was no way I wanted to have this conversation right now. Fast as I could, I spun around and went back inside, closing the door between the two of us and turning out the kitchen light so she would get the message.

The phone rang just when I figured it would—thirteen minutes after I shut the door on Amy.

"You mean your father got some girl pregnant when he was a kid?" she said as soon as I picked up.

"Well, not a kid, but when he was a resident at a hospital in New York."

"Before he was married to your mother?"

"Of course before he was married to my mother. Before he even *knew* my mother," I said.

"So how'd he get here, this Zachary person? How long's he going to stay?"

"Forever. He's going to stay forever, at least till he grows up and moves away." I took the phone into the big downstairs closet with its boots and coats and tennis rackets and Rollerblades, settling onto the floor and telling Amy how suddenly I had this brother I didn't need or want. I told her how he'd moved into the third floor and how my father had taken him shopping and how they came in with all these Gap bags and how I didn't think Dad even knew where the Gap *was*. I told her about the adoption that hadn't happened and how Zachary's mother had died and, oh, everything.

"Oh wow," said Amy, when I was finished. "I feel so sorry for him."

Zachary

If this is what being in this family's like, forget it. It's the meals that are the real bummers, like *Night of the Living Dead* or *Tales from the Crypt*: zombie-ville. Talk about cause and effect. It doesn't take an Einstein to figure out that I'm the cause that brought about the effect.

I've got to hand it to her though—every time we sit down to eat, Winnie tries to dredge up a conversation. Tottie, on the other hand, sulks, and the father sits at his end of the table and looks about five inches away from where I actually am. And Brian talks nonstop. About a bunch of kids named Teddy and Andy and Sammy and Ryan, about T-ball and the Baltimore Orioles and the Ravens and even brussels sprouts and how he hates them.

The brussels sprouts. If the strain of the other three gets to me, life with Motormouth is almost worse.

Mom had a real thing about meals. They were a coming together, she always said. A time for unwinding and recharging and firing up for the next round. Sometimes they were for zoning out, doing crossword puzzles, reading, or checking out the sports page. And if it was quiet, it was a noisy quiet.

I'm not even sure what I expected here. Some kind of great bonding scene? The whole long-lost father-and-son thing? The world according to Steven Spielberg.

That first night, after supper, he took me down to the bus station to get my backpack out of the storage locker where I'd stashed it. Brian came too, which actually worked well because having him along totally wiped out the need for conversation. At least until his father told him to cool it and let someone else talk, and for the rest of the way he, Dr. David Edward Flannigan, pointed the sights out for me. It was dark by then so all I had to do was say "Yeah," "Sure," "Uh-huh," with the occasional "Is that right?" thrown in.

They dropped me at the front door and I went inside, breathing the familiar bus-station smells and feeling that maybe this was where I belonged. I retrieved my backpack and stood mentally tallying the money I had left, all the while staring at the people slouched on chairs and benches. I deducted the cost of a ticket to Anywhere and tried to think how I'd go about getting a job and finding a place to stay. There was another door on the far side of the station, and I had just shrugged into my backpack when I felt a tug on my sleeve. Motormouth was looking up at me.

"Dad said to tell you the policeman made him move and he's driving around the block, but he'll be right back to pick us up, so come on. And maybe we can get ice cream on the way home."

No sooner were we back in the car than the travelogue resumed.

". . . Just detour a bit . . . see the sights . . . Harborplace and in the distance Federal Hill . . . Charles Street and now the Washington Monument . . . Johns Hopkins University on the left . . ."

Church was never a big thing for Mom and me. Once when I was about eight, she took me to the Friends' Meeting House, which seemed to be filled with a lot of people sitting around waiting for something to happen. Mom said afterward that they were waiting to be moved to speak and then they'd get up and say something. Trouble was, she said, that the wear and tear on her, wondering what *I* might be tempted to say, was more than she felt like dealing with, so we never went back. I was more unpredictable in those days. Come to think of it, something like Brian is now.

That about did it for the church scene, except for a couple of bar mitzvahs I went to in middle school, and the only things I remember about them are the yarmulkes and that the ceremonies were long.

When my mother got really sick, the hospice people sent a chaplain who, even though he was a Presbyterian minister, was pretty cool—which I never thought a minister would be. He came every week, and more often at the end, and they would talk. Sometimes I'd be there and sometimes not. The thing is, I never thought of them as actually *praying*, but maybe that's what praying is sometimes. Afterward, when she died, he conducted the funeral and even gave me his address and phone number and told me to keep in touch.

I've got an idea my mother would've liked it if I had called him, at least once. But I also think she would have understood why I never did.

Anyway, in this house everybody goes to church on Sunday morning. I found that out when the doctor showed up in my room, still not looking directly at me, and said, "We'll be leaving for church in half an hour, in case you want to join us."

I didn't, but then I remembered the old *when in Rome*

thing and crawled out of bed and rooted in my backpack for something to wear. There wasn't much to pick from, and what there was didn't exactly fit anymore. Toward the end, neither Mom nor I was much into shopping.

Church happened, and afterward we went back to the house and had one of those wonderfully relaxing meals with everyone looking as if they were shoving E. coli or botulism in with their scrambled eggs. I felt trapped and wanted out of there, but I didn't know where to go. I wondered what Tony and the guys back in Ohio were doing. I wondered what I was going to do all day, and for the rest of my life.

Winnie to the rescue. She suggested that the doctor take me to the mall and get me some clothes. Actually, Winnie's pretty cool. And oddly enough, I think my mother would have liked her. I can almost see them sitting at our old kitchen table, talking and sipping that skanky herbal tea Mom used to like. Besides, Winnie knows a heck of a lot more about being a father than *he* does.

I don't think the doctor was thrilled with Operation Shopping, but Brian-the-buffer came along, which definitely helped. He and I talked baseball the whole way to the mall—mostly the Orioles. But hey, if the O's are my new hometown team, I figured I'd better get informed. I'm beginning to think Brian has the makings of an okay kid.

We went to the Gap and a couple of other stores and got jeans and shirts and a pair of khakis. Before we left, the doctor asked if there was anything else I needed.

Underwear. Socks. A bus ticket to Ohio. My old life back, I wanted to say, but didn't.

On the way home the doctor harrumphed his way into what was obviously *a serious conversation*. "Well, Zachary, I made a few phone calls last night and this morning, and I'm waiting for one more person to get back to me. But I think it'll all work out—think we can get you into Xavier High School."

"Xavier?"

"Yes, it's one of the best boys' high schools here in town. Great school, actually, where they give you a terrific education. It's where I went, where I hope Brian will go."

"Boys' school?" Where was Jessica Finan when I needed her most?

"Don't let that worry you," he said. "At Xavier there's plenty of interaction with the girls' schools in the area. Dances, plays, community service projects."

Interaction? I thought. Community service projects? I let that one go by and concentrated on the Xavier part. "Doesn't Xavier mean it's Catholic?" I asked. "Because I'm not one."

"Don't worry about that. No one's going to try and pressure you. In fact, I don't even know their policy about non-Catholics taking religion courses. There may well be an alternative. We'll look into that. Anyway, check the school out and see what you think, and then we'll talk. Okay?"

"Yeah, sure. But I've always gone to public schools. Mom really believed in them."

"Oh, I believe in them too—but I think you'll like Xavier."

End of conversation.

Trouble was, I couldn't figure where this guy was coming from. He went through that whole "This is my son" thing with the neighbor this morning, and obviously did a major string-pulling job to get me into his school of choice in the spring of third year. But the whole time he was doing all that, he still made me feel like a walking foot fungus. Weird.

Once we got home I headed upstairs, but not before the doctor reminded me about the list of things I needed sent from Ohio. "I want to get started on that," he said, "soon as you get it down on paper."

I flopped down on the bed, looking around the room and thinking how, with a little effort, I could turn it into a really cool space. Eventually I reached for paper and pencil, trying to think of what to put down. Stereo, CDs, clothes. The computer, of course, and maybe the TV from the living room. I wasn't sure how much I could ask to have sent. Wasn't sure who was supposed to pay for it to get here. And once all this stuff arrived, was I really saying I was here to stay?

I could be on my own, I thought. I *should* be on my own.

But you didn't get on that bus last night, came a niggling voice inside my head. *And it wasn't all because of Brian.*

Tottie

"I feel sorry for him, too," said Ellen the next day at lunch. This was the first time we'd all had a chance to talk since I'd told Amy the Zachary story the night before. I deliberately hadn't asked her not to tell anyone else (except parents, which goes without saying) because I figured that if she passed it along to Ellen and Margaret, then I wouldn't have to. But I did, because there was Ellen saying she felt sorry for Zachary, and Margaret nodding in a me-too kind of way.

"You feel sorry for HIM?" I shrieked, then quickly lowered my voice when almost everybody in the cafeteria turned to look at me. "You feel sorry for *him*?" I whispered. "Thanks a lot."

"Yes, but his *mother* died and he had to come to some city he's probably never been to before and live with a bunch of people he doesn't even know and—" Ellen's face wobbled and she bit down on her lip, as if at any minute she might dissolve into tears.

"And he got from Ohio to here, on his own. Like *Lassie Come-Home* or something," said Margaret, still nodding her head.

"But it's not home. Not *his* home anyway. That's my point." My voice sounded like air hissing out of a balloon. "And now all of a sudden I have this person living in my house who's some kind of a brother and I'm supposed to be all thrilled about it—is that what you guys think?"

"He might be nice," said Margaret, and for a minute I wanted to kick her.

"Yeah, and he might be an ax murderer, too," I said.

"No way." Amy waved her half-eaten turkey sandwich in front of my face and said, "There's no way Dr. Flannigan's son could be an ax murderer, or even a nerd."

"And besides," said Ellen, "not one of us ever had an older brother and we always said we wanted one. You know, somebody to introduce us to all his good-looking friends who will then take us on dates—when our parents let us *go* on dates."

"He doesn't have any friends," I said, reaching over for one of Amy's chips. "Not in Baltimore, at least. And I should have known better than to hope for sympathy from you all."

They sat back and looked at me for a minute, but if I'd expected them to grovel or say they were eternally sorry and of course I was right from the start—it didn't happen. Finally Ellen crossed her arms and said, "The way I see it, your main worry is how to keep your mother from writing about this in one of her columns. In the newspaper. Which she probably will." And which, weird as it may sound, had not yet occurred to me.

"She wouldn't," I said. "Even my mother, who writes about all the world's embarrassing moments, wouldn't do that."

Or would she? The words wormed their way into my brain and stayed there all afternoon. Through social studies and phys ed and even math.

"Mom!" I yelled as I tore into the house after school and headed straight upstairs to her study, where she was sitting and staring at the computer. "You wouldn't, would you?" I screeched, dropping my backpack.

"Wouldn't what?"

"Wouldn't ever—not in a million years—write about

Zachary in one of your columns. About him coming here and all that stuff, you know, with Dad," I said.

"Are you telling me what to write, Tottie? Is this censorship rearing its ugly head? Even *The Sun* doesn't tell me what not to do in my column." She looked up at me, all the while rubbing the mouse back and forth over the mouse pad, which is something she does when she's really agitated.

"Well, no," I said. "I'm not *telling* you what to do exactly—but you wouldn't, would you?"

"It's probably a moot point, because the way I feel now I'll never write again and I have to get something off to my editor by E-mail almost immediately." Mom stared at the mouse, at the screen, then at the mouse again.

"What about the Motherhood and Early Spring file?" I asked. A couple of years ago, when she was laid up with a broken ankle, Mom wrote several pieces on generic subjects and put them in what she called the Motherhood and Early Spring folder—to be used in the event of a catastrophe. Which, I could have told her yesterday, Zachary's coming actually was.

"That's what I'm doing now. I found a piece on the excitement of getting out into the garden, in early spring, but it sounds tired and I'm trying to spruce it up a bit."

My mother took off her glasses and rubbed her forehead. "It hasn't been a good day."

"What happened?" I asked.

"Well, nothing *happened* happened. It's just that I had to take Zachary out to Xavier to see what he thought of it—and what they thought of him—"

"What's for *him* not to like?" I said. "Though I can see where *they* might have a problem."

My mother ignored me, which she's sometimes pretty good at doing. "From there we had to go back to the mall because your father's idea of shopping doesn't include underwear and shoes and the blue shirts and another pair of khakis he'll need for Xavier," she said. And her tone of voice gave me the clue that this was a prime topic for one of those low-voiced conversations my parents sometimes have. Mostly behind closed doors. Anyway, she sighed and went on. "And by then it was way past lunchtime, so we stopped for something to eat—"

"I thought you thought this was such a terrific idea," I couldn't quite resist saying.

"I never used the word *terrific*," my mother said. Actually, she more or less snapped it. "I think I said it was the *right* thing to do, and it still is. Maybe it's just that I'm not used to teenage boys, but it's the talking that's hard. I mean, I'm sure Zachary's a great kid, but he doesn't say much. The more he didn't talk, the more I did until I ended up sounding like a blathering fool." She sighed again and turned back to the computer.

"Where is he now?"

"Outside. He offered to do some yard work and I handed him a rake and said, 'Go.' Then I ran up here and turned on the computer. Brian went home with Danny after school, and I'm going to need you to pick him up later on. And right now, I have to get some work done."

I went over to the window, separating the blinds and looking out at the backyard. "He's talking now," I said.

"Who?"

"Zachary."

"To whom?"

"Mrs. Batterton. She's got him trapped down at the far-back corner of the yard."

"Well, you know as well as I do that with Mrs. Batterton it's more listening than talking," said Mom.

"Yeah, except this looks like a two-way conversation to me." I made the space between the slats even wider and stared at Zachary, watching the way he moved his hands in time with how fast he seemed to be opening and closing his mouth. "Yes, definitely a two-way conversation."

My mother groaned and put her elbows on the computer table, dropping her head into her hands.

Serves him right, I thought. I can't think of a better welcome to the neighborhood than an afternoon with Mrs. B. I let go of the blinds and stepped back, savoring the idea of Zachary stuck with Mrs. Batterton, when a wave of panic swept over me. "Not Mrs. Batterton," I screeched. "She can get information out of a stone. She's better than the CIA or the FBI or—" I stumbled over the backpack I'd left lying on the floor and raced downstairs and into the kitchen, yanking open the back door and calling, "Hey, Zachary. Can you come here a minute?" Then I moved back into the room, so he'd have to come all the way in to see what I wanted.

"What's up?" he asked when he reached the back door.

"Nothing. I was just trying to rescue you is all."

"Rescue?" Zachary crinkled his forehead, and it was like some weird déjà vu moment with my father's face superimposed on top of this stranger's. "From what?"

I hesitated, torn between wanting Zachary to suffer the miseries of a conversation with Mrs. B. and not wanting her to hear all about my father and Susan Pearce.

"Not what. Who," I said, reaching into the fridge and taking out a bottle of cranberry juice. I poured myself a glass and shoved the bottle over to him. "You have to watch out for Mrs. Batterton. She can be mean as a snake, not to mention nasty and nosy. You're better off staying away from her, coming in if she goes out, you know, in the yard, I mean."

"She seemed okay," said Zachary, helping himself to some juice.

" 'Okay'?" I asked.

"Well, harmless, anyway. She asked me about my mother."

Yeah, I just bet she did, I thought. And pretty soon she'll be up and down the block, spreading the word about our suddenly dysfunctional family. I could almost see her slobbering over it the same as her dog, Toby, slobbers over table scraps. "I can only imagine," I said.

"She wanted to know if my mom was a writer, too," said Zachary. "That's the first I knew about what Winnie does. What kind of stuff does she write?"

"Columns, for *The Sun*. About a lot of things, like family and all." I suddenly remembered the column I wanted my mother never to write, and I could feel my face start to burn.

"I gotta go," I said, grabbing the juice and putting it back in the refrigerator. "Brian went home after school with his friend Danny McKenny, and I think Mom wants me to walk over and get him." I turned and hurried out of the kitchen.

———————

It wasn't exactly a lie because I'd no sooner settled down with the phone to call Amy than Mom *did* ask me to go get Brian. When I got to Danny's, his mother said the boys were downstairs straightening up the playroom and why didn't I have some oatmeal-raisin cookies while I waited. I was halfway through my second one when Mrs. McKenny said, "Oh, Tottie, Brian tells me your older brother has come to stay. I just bet you all must be thrilled."

I choked and coughed and sort of gagged. My eyes watered and I began to wonder if I could actually die from inhaling cookie crumbs right there in the McKennys' kitchen. After what seemed like ages, I managed to catch my breath and squeak out, "Yeah, well I'm going to tell Brian he'd better hurry. But thanks for the cookies."

"You told Danny about Zachary?" I said, as Brian and I were walking home.

"Yep."

"How come?"

"How come not?"

"I mean, do you like him being here?" I asked.

"Yeah." Brian was suddenly into one-word answers.

"Why do you? Like him being here?"

"He's nice. And besides, I never had a brother and I need one."

"You never had a boa constrictor, either, but that doesn't mean you *need* one," I said.

Brian stopped and stood kicking at a tree root, making a kind of thumping sound. "I never wanted a boa constrictor," he said. "But I always did want a brother—and now I have one. Come on, let's go. I'm starving."

Zachary

I woke up on Monday morning to the sound of everybody yelling back and forth, the dog barking, a radio playing somewhere in the house, and, finally, a door slamming. By the time I got to the window, the doctor's car was already gone and Winnie and Tottie and Brian were piling into the other one.

Talk about the *Home Alone* kid. I stood there, even after they'd gone, caught by the sudden silence of the house and watching the flat-faced dog next door sniff his way along the fence. After that I took a shower, put on my new jeans and a shirt from the Gap, and started downstairs.

On the second floor, my feet went into detour mode. First I checked out Tottie's room, which, what with the old movie posters taped around the walls, wasn't bad. If she'd ditch the stuffed animals. Brian's room was a jumble of action figures and little-kid trophies and toy cars on every available surface. But the thing was, I was sure there was a purpose to it all and that if I moved even one, he'd spot it the minute he walked in the door. From there I went by Winnie's workroom—not much more than a large closet with a window—then on to the master bedroom, where I stopped just inside the doorway.

The dog was curled up on the unmade bed. He looked at me, and I looked at him. In the two days I'd been here, Punch and I hadn't exactly bonded. That may have had something to do with the fact that, except for Tony's yellow Lab and the mutt in the apartment downstairs who howled when the moon was full, dogs had never been a big part of my life. Back when I was six and started the I-want-a-pet routine, my mother pronounced herself allergic to all animal life, which may or may not have been the truth. Either way, it ended the discussion. Though she was a pushover in some regards, Mom could be pretty firm about other things.

Anyway, after eyeballing me for a couple of minutes, Punch rolled over on his back, waving his feet in the air and inviting a belly rub. I sat next to him on the bed, happy to oblige as I looked around the room, taking in the clutter of books on the bedside tables, the open closet door, the empty coffee mugs. I was able to track Tottie and Brian's lives in the pictures on tabletops and windowsills—at the beach, the amusement park, the top of the swing set; decked out for Easter and Halloween. I remembered the pictures my mom kept, mostly of the two of us. I thought of how, when she was getting worse, she'd ask for one and lie there, rubbing her thumb up and down along the frame.

All of a sudden I felt I shouldn't be in this room, and wanted out. "Come on, dog," I said, getting up. "Let's go find something to eat."

I'd just about made it to the kitchen when Winnie came in the back door. "Oh good, you're up," she said. "It occurred to me last night that there wasn't even a clock in that room. What would you like for breakfast? There's cereal in the cupboard over there, and bagels in the freezer, orange juice and milk in the fridge. Around here we pretty much fend for ourselves at breakfast and lunch—even Brian, with a little supervision.

"And by the way, David's made all the arrangements at Xavier, so once you're done and I've seen to things upstairs, we'll head out there. If that's okay with you."

Eating my Frosted Flakes, I wondered what she *thought* I was going to say. That no, it wasn't okay? I had other plans for the day? Was into being a dropout? Though I did wonder, as I zapped my bagel in the microwave, that if this whole Xavier business was such a big deal, where was the doctor? And why wasn't *he* here, doing the alma mater thing?

It was almost as though Winnie had read my mind, because we were no sooner in the car than she said, "You know, Dave really wanted to take you out and register you for school himself, but his office hours start early on Mondays. He'll definitely go with you tomorrow, though, and show you where to get the bus to come home and all that."

I concentrated on finding the end of my seat belt as I mumbled, "Yeah, well, I'm sorry you got stuck."

"Stuck?" said Winnie. "It's not stuck—it's the way we do things. And if I have a meeting or a deadline for a column looming, he takes over with the kids. Tottie and Brian spent a lot of time hanging around Dave's office waiting room when they were younger."

What do you expect from the Cleavers? a part of me thought. And then a ton more thoughts came piling in. Like how my mother's whole life had been a juggling act, with no one to help, especially after Grandma died. How if she had had a meeting or a class or a paper due, it was tough toenails.

Hold it, I told myself. Mom didn't want to marry *him*, any more than he wanted to marry *her*. I knew it for a fact. But I was still pissed.

Xavier, which seemed to consist of a bunch of old stone buildings, was up on a hill, with grass and trees all around it.

"Wow," I said, the word slipping out before I could censor it.

"It is a nice campus," said Winnie, pulling into a parking lot in back. "And they've just opened a great new gym-and-pool complex. I haven't seen it, but Dave was out for the dedication."

Which any fool could tell meant the doctor was some big-deal contributor. Even I know that's who gets invited to those things. And it goes a long way to explain the strings he could pull for the son from nowhere.

There was a part of me right then that didn't want to go in, but we were already out of the car and heading for the door. Campus or no campus, I thought as Winnie led the way into the office, it smells like every other school I've ever been in. Odor of pencil shavings and stale air and sweat. Mostly sweat.

A mushroom-shaped woman looked up from her desk. "Mrs. Flannigan?" she said. "And Zach? We've been expecting you. Why don't you sit right here and we'll get some of this paperwork out of the way, then Father Connor will meet with you both." She handed me a piece of paper, saying, "You get started on this one, Zach." Then she passed a bunch more to Winnie.

"I have my birth certificate," I said, reaching for my wallet.

"I don't need that," the Mushroom said. "I talked to someone at your school in Cincinnati early this morning and they've already faxed your records."

Talk about moving things right along.

I concentrated on the form in front of me, printing out my name: Zachary Alan Pearce. A cold and clammy feeling took hold of me. What if they expected me to be *Flannigan* here? What if they were just waiting to yank who I was out from under me? I put my pen down, then picked it up again.

Winnie looked over at me. "Is there a problem?"

I shrugged and she leaned closer, to see what I had written. "That's who you are, Zachary. That's who you are," she said.

After that, things just seemed to get done. The Mushroom Lady did her thing. Winnie and I did ours. Forms were filled out and signed and passed from one of us to the other. Then, as if on cue, a door opened and a large man with a red face and steel-gray hair and steel-gray eyes came in.

"Winnie, it's good to see you again," he said, holding out a hand to her.

"You too, Father," she said. "And this is—"

"Zach," the priest said, coming across to shake my hand. "I'm Father Anton Connor. Welcome to Xavier." And with some kind of sleight of hand, we were down the hall and in his office, sitting across from him.

"You've had a tough time, Zach, and I'm sorry," Father Connor said. He looked right at me when he spoke, not even blinking, and those few words seemed to say more than anyone else had said to me since I left Ohio.

"Yes, sir," I said. "And thank you." And straight off, I filed him away in my head along with the Presbyterian minister as an okay guy. Some people you just know about.

He picked up the forms and riffled through them. "Ahhh, ZAP. Does anyone ever call you that?" he asked.

"No, not really. Except my mom sometimes, when she wanted to bug me."

"We'll try not to bug you here, then," the priest said, smiling and leaning back in his chair. "Now this has all got to be overwhelming for you, but there must be some questions you want to ask—about Xavier, or what to expect from us. What we'll expect from you."

"I'm not a Catholic," I said. "That's the main thing. So—what would I do here?"

"Be in good company," Father Connor said. "Twelve percent of our students are non-Catholics, and we have Muslims, Hindus, as well as a mixed bag of Protestants. We do require all our students to attend religion classes, but you'll find they consist of Old Testament studies, World Religions, and courses in basic values."

"Is that okay, Zachary?" asked Winnie, turning to look at me.

Like I was really going to say I wasn't into values?

"Think you can handle that?" the priest said.

"Yes, sure," I said, nodding.

"Good." Father Connor seemed to propel himself up out of his chair. "Winnie, why don't you make yourself comfortable here for a few minutes while I give Zach the ten-cent tour. Tomorrow we'll have a couple of the boys really show him around."

I followed him down the hall, around a corner, and then around another one. The walls along the way were lined with class pictures that were all pretty much the same, and all different. The year of graduation was in the center of each, and that, in turn, was surrounded by head shots of the individual boys in the class. Partway down the last hall, Father Connor stopped, reaching up to tap on the glass of one of them, saying, "Recognize anyone?"

My own face looked back at me. My knees threatened to give out and I could only nod.

"It's an amazing likeness," Father Connor said. He shoved his hands into his pockets and started on down the hall, then stopped and turned to me. "I wouldn't be doing my job if I didn't say this to you—so here it is. You may just surprise yourself and like this place," he said. "So give us a chance, Zach. For your sake—and your father's."

The rest of the tour went by in a blur. The library, the cafeteria, the science labs. By the time we made our way back to his office, my head was stuffed with facts about schedules, required courses, and a dress code that Father Connor described as "low-key." Which basically meant khakis instead of jeans, and a shirt and tie.

If I was confused before, by the time Winnie and I were back in the car my head was a real mess. As far as I could tell, Xavier was an okay school. The boys we passed on our tour seemed like regular guys, and I'd already given Father Connor a thumbs-up. And as far as I could figure, it'd be cool to go there.

So what was my hang-up?

"It doesn't seem right," I heard myself saying out loud. "Getting into that school like this. Pulling strings and all. That's the way it had to've been."

"In some ways you're right," said Winnie. She leaned

back against the seat and looked over at me. "I under-stand how you feel, and David would, too. But the better you get to know him, you'll find that this is totally out of character. It's the kind of thing he never does, which ought to give you some indication of how much he wants it for you. How much he wants to *do* it for you.

"And let me tell you this, Zachary," she went on. "Xavier is no slouch school. Dave may have gotten you in, but it's up to you to *stay* in. Mess up and you're out on your ear."

From there we went to the mall and got the rest of the stuff I needed for school, then on to one of those what-do-we-talk-about-now meals in the food court. All during lunch I kept having this feeling that there was more Win-nie wanted to say to me. I wasn't sure, but—something about the doctor? Like how this wasn't easy for him ei-ther? Maybe how it was even downright hard?

One thing I've never been good at is the empathy thing. The whole walking-a-mile-in-some-guy's-moccasins deal. So the closest I could come that day in the mall was con-ceding to myself at least that well, yeah, maybe I had de-livered a real blast from the past. Maybe I had.

Tottie

I sometimes wonder if the trouble with our house is that it's too civilized. That the trouble with the people in our family is that *they're* too civilized. I once told my mother that we were all positively loaded with inhibitions, and she said inhibitions had nothing to do with it—that there was a way to act and a way not to act. Then she wrote a whole column about it. And won an award.

I used to think it would be incredibly liberating if we all went around slamming doors and hurling pot lids at one another, until once last year when I went home to dinner with a girl named Sylvie Rogers so we could work on our science project together. Her mother and father sniped and snarled at each other all through the meal, and suddenly, just when we were starting in on apple pie with cheese, her mother stood up and threw a glass of ice water at her father. Not the glass—just the ice and water. And for only a fraction of a second I thought, *Hey, cool. She wanted to do it and she did it.* Then I looked at poor Mr. Rogers with water dripping off his hair and an ice cube resting on his chest, and Mrs. Rogers with her mean, twisted face, and Sylvie, who was biting her lip to keep from crying, and then down at my plate because it made me feel crawly to look at any one of them. That's when I knew that maybe civilized wasn't entirely bad.

Which, as I've already said, our family certainly is. Including the older generation. Or maybe that's where it came from.

Anyway, Nanny and Granddad arrived before dinner on Wednesday of that first Zachary-week. Brian and I were watching at the window in the den, the way we always do when our grandparents are coming, each one of us hoping to be the first to spot the car. Except that Brian kept running back to the table where Zachary was trying to teach him to play chess.

"They're here," I yelled, as the car swung into the driveway. "Come on, Brian. *Our* grandparents are here." I leaned sort of hard on the *our* part, hoping Zachary would get the message and stay in the den fiddling with the chess set.

It almost worked, too, except that Brian got all the way

to the door, then stopped and went back, saying, "Hurry up, Zach. Nanny and Granddad are here."

Zachary got up, and without looking at either one of us, shrugged his shoulders and followed.

When we got to the kitchen, Nanny and Granddad were just coming in the back door. "Well, here they are— our favorite Baltimore grandchildren," said Granddad, putting down the suitcases and rubbing his hands together.

"But we're your *only* Baltimore grandchildren," I said. "The others live in Topeka."

"Oh, is that right?" my grandfather said, in fake surprise. It was a kind of dumb routine we did every time they came for a visit, but if we hadn't done it things would've felt weird, like starting to march on the wrong foot or something.

"Well, Tottie," said Nanny, as she gave me a kiss. "Well, Brian," as she gave him a kiss. "And Zachary." Then my very own grandmother leaned forward and gave *him* a kiss. As if he'd been lined up there with her Baltimore grandchildren maybe forever.

Granddad came along behind her, hugging me and shaking hands with the boys. By this time Nanny was reaching into a plastic bag and pulling out the books we could always count on her bringing. There was a book about mummies for Brian, a mystery for me—and a story of an expedition to the top of Mount Everest for Zachary. That's when I gave my mother the raised-eyebrow look that *I* know *she* knew meant, "How'd you brainwash them like this?" Instead of raising her eyebrows back, she just smiled sweetly and *suggested* that Zachary and I carry the suitcases up to the guest room. Civilized, huh?

Just for the heck of it, and because my grandparents were unpacking and getting ready for dinner, I checked the thesaurus on the shelf next to Mom's desk to see if I could come up with a better word than *civilized* to describe what we were. The thing I like about a thesaurus is that it's kind of like being on a sitting-still treasure hunt, with one word (or clue) leading to another. First, I looked up *civilized*, which sent me in the direction of *tasteful*, *improved*, and *learned*. I scratched *learned* straightaway because our family isn't any more intelligent than anybody else's. I checked under *tasteful* and found *elegant*, *refined*, *polished* (a real laugh with Brian in the house), and *discriminating*, which we're obviously not, since we've just let a perfect stranger move in. From there I went on to *improved* and found *enhanced*, *perfected*, and *changed for the better.*

That was when I flipped back to the index and wrote NOT across the original entry for *civilized*. Mom never freaks out about writing in books as long as it's what she calls a serious annotation. In fact, she even wrote a piece about the messages she's found in secondhand books, so I figured I could defend my *not* if I had to. Meanwhile, I was just about to tackle *inhibition* when my mother called for me to come and help put dinner on the table.

As soon as we sat down to eat, Nanny made a tactical error by asking Brian what was new, and half a meal later he was still talking.

"This is fast becoming a filibuster, son," said Dad, reaching over to push Brian's glass away from the edge of the table.

"He means let somebody else talk," I said, giving Brian a poke under the table.

"Oh. Okay," he said, which didn't exactly help, because what he did then was answer everybody else's questions.

When Nanny asked me how Margaret, Ellen, and Amy were, Brian said, "Bo-ring. All they do is talk on the phone."

When Granddad asked Zachary how he liked Baltimore and whether he was interested in any extracurricular activities, Brian said, "He likes it a lot and I'm trying to talk him into playing lacrosse."

And when Nanny asked my mom what she was planning for her garden this year, Brian piped up with, "Mrs.

Battle-ax was looking over the fence today, and I'll bet she's going to turn the grass into straw."

That was when my father crinkled his forehead and said in his we've-let-you-get-away-with-this-but-now-it's-going-to-stop voice, "Brian, that's enough!"

Actually, I hadn't minded Brian's babbling because it gave me a chance to observe my family. Mostly my father, though that had to be done sort of sideways, because ever since hearing about him and Susan Pearce and baby Zachary, I hadn't been all that interested in looking at him eyeball to eyeball. I was curious to see whether, sitting at the dinner table with his wife's parents, he'd act even the teeniest, tiniest bit embarrassed. He didn't.

Hey, I wanted to shout, is this the same person who once wrote an article in some pediatric journal about how kids today are surrounded by too much permissiveness? And whatever happened to the old idea of sex *after* marriage? The word *hypocrite* came to mind, and I made a mental note to check that in Mom's thesaurus.

I studied my grandparents, who, I happen to know, really really like my father, trying to see if they were acting cold or distant or totally disillusioned. They weren't.

I skipped over Brian, holding forth on what happened when Punch almost caught a squirrel, and over Zachary, who was sitting there with my father's look-alike face, eating spinach lasagna like some kind of windup toy in the *on* mode. I went on to my mother, who seemed definitely preoccupied, which, Mom being Mom, could've been because she was wondering if the lasagna was as good as it should have been, or if the strawberry-rhubarb pie turned out okay, or maybe even about a column she had to write.

All this observation took me up to Dad giving Brian the bushy eyebrow treatment, and I had to start paying attention.

"Your grandmother and I'll go over to Washington one day while you're in school," Granddad was saying. "And then up to Longwood Gardens. But have you kids decided what you want to do on Saturday, for our special day?"

Our special day is a no-parents-allowed time we go out with Nanny and Granddad when we get to pick the place, though they have veto power, which explains why we've only eaten at the Hard Rock Café once and never at ESPN Zone.

"The aquarium," shouted Brian. "Or the Science Center."

"Fells Point," I said. "And the water taxi."

"Well," said Nanny, getting up to help Mom clear the table, "I guess we'll have to wait and see what the weather's like on Saturday, but wherever we go, Zachary, we want you to come with us."

I looked at Zachary, who raised his eyebrows and crinkled his forehead and said, "Well, yeah, thank you but . . . I mean I have school stuff and all . . . I'd better just not—"

"Oh, but we insist," said Nanny from the doorway. "Our day out with the children is one of our favorite times and we want you to be a part of it."

I grabbed the lasagna dish off the table and followed my grandmother into the kitchen. "You're not *his* Nanny," I whispered.

She put the plates on the counter and turned around, stepping on my toe as she did. "Oh dear, I am sorry. Was that your foot?" my grandmother said.

". . . And there are sharks and a dolphin show and an octopus and everything," said Brian as we headed downtown Saturday morning. "But at the Science Center there's an IMAX movie."

"It's too nice a day for either indoor fish *or* a movie," I said, scrunching my body up as small as it would go, because I was stuck between Brian and Zachary in the backseat of Granddad's car.

"I think Tottie's right," said Nanny.

"But all Fells Point is is a bunch of stores and restaurants," Brian broke in.

Nanny held her hand up to him and went on as if he hadn't spoken. "So what we'll do is split up. Brian, you and your granddad go do what you want. Tottie and I'll ride the water taxi over to Fells Point. And Zachary, you get to pick which you'd rather do. Okay?"

I froze. I held my breath till there was a pounding in my head, and I almost didn't hear Zachary say, "Oh, either the aquarium or the Science Center is okay with me." Then I let my breath out all at once, not really caring if he heard the whoosh or not.

After we parked the car, we walked over to Harborplace and picked a spot for us to meet at four o'clock. Then Granddad, Brian, and Zachary headed for the Science Center, and Nanny and I got the water taxi for Fells Point. Fells Point is this really cool place that's maybe the oldest part of Baltimore. The streets are narrow and cobblestone, and the houses are just narrow. There are bunches of shops and restaurants and art galleries with a market on the square in the middle.

One of the best things about my grandmother is that she is always ready for lunch, and says that—when it's a special occasion—dessert is an integral part of any meal. As soon as we got off the water taxi, we headed for the nearest restaurant, taking a table by the window so we could watch the boats and the people and the light on the water. We had chicken-salad sandwiches and diet sodas and brownies à la mode. While half of me wanted to bring up the Zachary subject, the other half won out. I mean, why ruin a good meal?

When lunch was over, we wandered in and out of galleries and shops selling old books and funky clothes and teddy bears and brassware and stuff from ships. We walked through the market, breathing in the pickle and sausage and bread smells, and sat on a bench outside drinking bottled water and watching pigeons and seagulls and a yellow dog sleeping in the sun. I was sort of spacing out when I heard my grandmother say, "Zachary seems like a nice young man."

"I still think it could be a trick," I said, jerking back to the present. "One of those gigantic hoaxes you read about in the paper all the time where somebody worms his way into a house and holds an entire family hostage."

"Our papers in North Carolina must not cover those stories," Nanny said. "I don't think I've seen a one."

"You know what I mean."

"And you know, as well as I do, that your parents have checked his story thoroughly," my grandmother said. "And what I see is a nice young man."

"It could be an act," I said, slouching down and pushing my heels into the ground in front of me.

"Somewhat bereft, but—"

"Don't tell me *you* feel sorry for him, too?" I said, suddenly sitting up straight.

"Don't *you*?" Nanny asked.

I didn't answer but sat there with my arms crossed over my chest, watching the yellow dog breathe in and out.

"Tottie?"

"Don't you care about my father? What he did? Aren't you disillusioned? Disappointed, on account of he's not the person you thought he was?"

"Your father is exactly the man I thought he was—a caring husband and father and a wonderful doctor," Nanny said.

"But he—"

"Tell me something, Tottie. Are you planning to get to your father's age without ever making a mistake? Because that's a pretty good trick, if you can pull it off. Have you given this any thought from your father's point of view?"

"Well, I—it's—"

"Because, you know, I'm sure there's a lot about this situation that Dave regrets. You're old enough to understand that none of this is easy for him, or for your mother, but they're trying to do what they think has to be done."

"It's not exactly easy for me," I said under my breath.

"Or you either," Nanny said, reaching over to squeeze

my hand. "Or Brian. Or Zachary, who's probably the person this is the hardest for. Don't forget that." She looked at her watch and got up. "We'd better go over and wait for the water taxi," she said. "But promise me something—that you'll talk to your father and tell him how you feel and what bothers you the most. And that you'll stop those silly sidelong glances. Okay?"

Yeah, sure, *Hi Dad*, I thought. *Let me tell you how I feel about the thing you had with that Susan Pearce person, and how all this time there's been this kid, and how if I'd read about him in a book I'd feel sorry for him but because he's real and your son and my partway brother, I somehow can't. Let's talk about that.*

I got up and followed Nanny across the street to the dock, wondering how come all these really intelligent grownup people I know think it's so easy to talk to parents. Even basically okay ones like mine.

Zachary

Winnie was right. The doctor did take me to school the next day, but if she had any thought about this being a great bonding experience—forget it. What I did get, between here and there, was a major lecture on the history of Xavier High School. Its found*ing*, its found*ers*, and the move from the city to the stone buildings on the hill, all well before the doctor's time. We're talking old here.

Then there was the Xavier network. Alumni as a part of the community. Xavierites in the judiciary, the medical profession, the world of commerce. It wasn't long before my eyes began to glaze over. Was this guy for real, I wondered, or did I just, somehow, press his pompous button?

"Are they big in sports?" I broke in, somewhere along the way.

This led to a full five minutes on the great Thanksgiving football tradition, the game between Xavier and their arch rival, Norwood. "Tottie's not much interested, but I've taken Brian the last few years. You'll have to come along sometime," he said.

Which may or may not have been an invitation. With the doctor, it's hard to tell.

The one practical piece of information I managed to pick up was where to catch the bus back to the house.

When we got to school, the Mushroom Lady was ready with my schedule and there were two guys, Jordan and Tom, waiting to take me to my first class.

"If we go now, there'll be time to fill you in before homeroom," the one named Jordan said.

"Sounds good to me," I said. I turned to the doctor. "See you, and thanks for the ride."

"Well now, Zachary, you have a great day," he answered, all the while fixing his attention on the wilted fern on the corner of the Mushroom's desk.

"Whoa—do you look like your dad!" Jordan said as we were cutting across the quadrangle to another building.

"Yeah, man. No way he could deny you," said Tom. That didn't even rate a comment on my part, and in a minute he went on, saying, "Now we'd better educate you on the really important stuff—like watch out for Kelly in chemistry. He thinks he personally owns the chem lab and that every broken test tube comes right out of his hide."

"And Morrison, in history—if he says write three pages, he means five," put in Jordan, stopping outside the next building. "But three pages for Clifton in English means three pages and not a word more."

"Now Richardson, who teaches third-year French, is basically okay—except when he's not," said Tom. "But then, I guess as teachers go, they're an okay lot."

"As long as you know the pitfalls," Jordan threw in. "Now come on, so we can introduce you to some of the guys before homeroom."

I don't want to get carried away here, but I might go so far as to say that my first day at Xavier was the best day I'd had since my mom got sick. Either Jordan or Tom, sometimes both, was in each of my classes. In fact, they stuck to me like chewing gum, helping me navigate the lunchroom and the locker room. They took me to the bookstore and pointed out the stuff I *didn't* need, and even explained how I should walk up a block after school, so I could catch the bus before it got to the mob waiting at the regular stop.

I met more people than I'll ever remember. At least for now.

A bunch of kids asked where I'd lived before.

"Ohio," I said.

"Cool. You like it here? In Baltimore?"

"Yeah, sure. At least I guess I will," I answered over and over again, though I had serious reservations about whether that was ever going to happen.

There was a lot of sports talk: Maryland basketball, the Orioles' spring training, and especially lacrosse, which seems to be a big deal here, but wasn't where I came from. But even with all that, I didn't get the impression that the place had too much of a jock mentality.

I went home fairly psyched and not at all ready for Motormouth, who came knocking at my bedroom door as I settled down with my history text.

"Want to play ball?" he asked, coming to stand beside me.

"Can't," I said. "I've got to do history."

"Want to play ball after that?"

"Sorry, kid, but after history comes math. How about you—don't you have homework?"

"We were supposed to—we always have homework, except today right after lunch Mrs. Porter, she's our teacher, had to leave and this substitute came in," Brian explained. "And substitutes are good on account of they never know about stuff like homework and spelling tests, so we were pretty sure we wouldn't have any—homework, not spelling tests—except this dumb girl named Sissy raised her hand and said we should, but then the bell rang and there wasn't any more time and so we don't."

I was drowning in second-grade trivia, and desperate measures were called for. "Look, Brian," I said, standing up and ushering him over to the door, "you let me get this work finished, and once I'm done I'll come down and teach you a really cool game. Okay?"

"What game?" he asked.

I shook my head and put my finger to my lips. "This game is so cool I can't even tell you about it yet."

Which explains how I ended up teaching chess to a seven-year-old. "The most important thing you have to understand about this game," I said to Brian as I put the board on the family-room table after dinner, "the *absolutely* most important thing, is that you have to be quiet when you play it. Watch a chess match sometime and you'll see—we're talking *silence*, man."

Brian nodded.

Not to say there wasn't a method in my madness.

For starters, I identified the pieces. "One king, one queen," I said. And Brian nodded again. "Two bishops, two knights, two rooks." Another nod. "And eight pawns."

He sat studying them for a while, then named them

back for me, mouthing the words as if afraid to break the code of silence.

"Now the object of the game is to capture the other guy's king," I said. "But first I have to show you how to set up the board." Brian watched what I did, then swept the pieces off and did it himself.

We're talking smart.

I was just about to launch into how to play the game when the doctor came by, leaned over Brian's shoulder, and said, "Well, you boys playing chess? That's great."

"Shhhhhh," whispered Brian, turning to look at his father. "You have to be quiet to play. Zach said so."

The doctor looked at me and raised his eyebrows, and I raised mine back, and for a minute it was like some total weirds-ville communication. "Sorry, I forgot," he whispered, turning back to Brian. "But right now it's your bedtime. Maybe you can play again tomorrow."

Brian and I were back at the chessboard the next day when Winnie's parents, the kids' grandparents, arrived. If I'd had any trouble grasping that concept, Tottie made sure I got the point with her "*our* grandparents" this, and "*our* grandparents" that. I didn't have any illusions that the Cleavers were even remotely thrilled by my being there, but it was definitely Tottie who was the most freaked. Which didn't bother me all that much. I mean if Amazon.com had been in the business of offering sisters, she's not what I'd've ordered either.

I could tell from the minute the grandparents walked in the door that they were going on my okay-from-the-start list, along with Father Connor and the Presbyterian minister. They—the grandparents—were both tall and slim and looked like the kind of couple you see on television, walking the beach and touting vitamin A, B, or C. The cool part, though, was that they let me know from the get-go that finding an extra kid in their daughter's house was fine by them. They even brought me a book.

One thing about having them there—the atmosphere at the dinner table was definitely improved. Except for Tottie of the evil eye. For a change there was real conversation—after the Brian monologue, that is—and I even picked up some things I hadn't known. Like the fact that Winnie's column is a bigger deal than I'd realized, and that the doctor had written some kind of child-raising book, which made him an authority. Though you couldn't prove it by me.

Apparently there's some kind of family tradition here where "Nanny" and "Granddad" take the kids out for the day. If you ask me, this smacks too much of a grade-school field trip, but there was no way I could get out of it.

(Major digression: what was I supposed to call these people? Winnie was easy, as were Tottie and Brian. But the grandparents weren't *my* grandparents, yet I was having trouble with the Helen and Jack, which is what they suggested. And what about the doctor? What was I supposed to call *him*?)

But to get back to the field trip. Tottie and her grandmother took off for someplace called Fells Point and the rest of us went to the Science Center. After the IMAX movie, Brian got hung up in the dinosaur exhibit and the grandfather and I headed for the next area over, where they had this really impressive thing about the Hubble telescope. Turns out he knows a ton of stuff about space, which ended up making the whole experience incredibly fascinating and produced another good day.

Two in one week?

Mom would have been glad about that.

Tottie

I didn't talk to my father. Partly because no matter what my grandmother said, it wasn't that easy, and partly (mostly) because I didn't try. Up until that Saturday when Zachary arrived, my father had been a kind of knight on a horse or a pedestal or whatever it is that knights are up on. Then, in that one afternoon, he came crashing down—*and* grew these giant clunky clay feet. Which *my* father definitely wasn't supposed to have and made me feel as though I'd been living with an impostor all these years. And what can you say to an impostor?

Besides, once Nanny and Granddad left, even though we were still terribly civilized, we weren't quite *as* civilized. Or maybe it was that we all seemed to hole up in our own particular corners of the house.

My father mostly worked, and when he wasn't at the office or the hospital, he was in his den reading medical journals and papers and things. Judging by the amount of time my mother spent in her workroom, she must be at least a dozen columns ahead by now, and the Motherhood and Early Spring folder had probably grown to the size of a telephone book. When he wasn't at school, Zachary pretty much stayed on the third floor, except when he was in the backyard raking what looked like the same stuff over and over and sometimes even talking to Mrs. Batterton. Meanwhile, I always tried to be where my father and Zachary were *not*. And as for Brian, he was totally into playing chess with Zachary, but otherwise clueless about life in general.

When we all got together for breakfast or dinner or church on Sunday, we were 100 percent polite, and thorny and sort of distant. I spent a lot of time giving my father dirty looks—but only when he was facing the other way. It was along about then that I decided not to go to the father-daughter dinner at school this year.

The father-daughter dinner, which is held in the spring, could also be called the stepfather-stepdaughter dinner, the uncle-niece dinner, the older brother–younger sister dinner, or any-other-combination-you-can-think-of dinner. It's one of those things that sound positively dorky— and is actually outstanding. The last two years Ellen,

Amy, Margaret, and I (and our fathers) all went together and sat together and ate together at a big round table right in the center of the room. We, the daughters, wore little corsages made of carnations and baby's breath our dads gave us and spent our time looking at what everybody else had on and laughing at the way Jennifer Lenski's father did the limbo. Our fathers talked about baseball and lacrosse. Somewhere between the chicken Parmesan and the chocolate marshmallow sundaes, a photographer came around and we had our pictures taken with Amy, Ellen, Margaret, and me sitting on lined-up chairs and our fathers standing in back. I keep those pictures in my room, on the dresser, except now I've let stuff pile up in front of them so I won't have to look.

The flyers for this year's dinner were given out in homeroom on a Friday morning. As soon as I saw what it was, I scrunched it down deep in my pocket until I got a chance to go in the girls' bathroom and read it all the way through in private. The whole time I was reading it, I got that creepy-crawly feeling I'd been getting a lot lately. When I got to the bottom, the fill-in-this-form-if-you're-coming part, I tore it into a million pieces. Then I flushed them down the toilet and devoted the rest of the day to trying to keep my friends from talking about the dinner or avoiding them altogether. I even went to the library after school when I didn't have to.

I knew I couldn't completely escape, and on Sunday afternoon Amy called. "So, what are you wearing to the father-daughter dinner?" she asked without even saying hello.

"I don't know," I said, adding a bunch of mumbly jumbly stuff into the phone, which didn't slow Amy down a bit.

"My mom says I can get a new dress, and I bet your mother'll let you get one, too, and then maybe the four of us can go shopping together. But if that doesn't work out, my mother says maybe Rosalia can take just you and me. And that might be even better because Rosalia doesn't exactly *care* about things—like how short a skirt is or how wide the straps are on things. What do you think?"

"I think I'm not going," I said. "I know I'm not going."

"What do you *mean* you're not going?" screeched Amy. "Of course you're going."

"No, I'm not."

"Why?"

"Because I can't. Because—I mean—I think— Because my father's got something really major to do that night. A kind of meeting. A medical thing. You know, something totally important."

"There isn't anything more important than the father-daughter dinner," said Amy. "Besides, I'll bet if you told him his thing was on the same night, he'd change it. Did you ask?"

"It's not just him. I mean, it's this huge event at a downtown hotel with hundreds of people going, and they're not going to change it for some middle-school father-daughter dinner," I said, half beginning to believe there *was* an event my father had to attend.

"He could miss it then. The medical thingie, I mean."

"Not *my* father. Not Dr. David 'Conscientious' Flannigan," I said, surprised at the sting to my words. "So that's the way it is—we're not going."

"Well, come with us then. My dad'll take you. He'll even bring you a corsage," said Amy.

"Thanks," I said, "but no thanks. It's okay, really." By the time we hung up I was feeling sort of sorry for myself, all on account of this important, major, totally made-up event.

I knew it was going to happen, and it did—they were at my door within an hour. Amy, Ellen, and Margaret were lined up across the back step with Margaret's dog, Fang, in tow, which I knew right off was their excuse for why we'd have to talk outside. That's because Fang intensely dislikes Punch, and Mom says that since it's Punch's house,

Fang is persona non grata. Which means *not welcome.*

"Come on out," said Margaret, as soon as I opened the door. "I got stuck walking the beast, so I thought we could all go."

"Yeah, okay. As soon as I grab a jacket and tell my mother I'm leaving," I said. "But I'm still not going to the dinner."

"Why not?" said Ellen when we were down the driveway and on the sidewalk. "I mean, even if your dad has to go to this super-important other thing, you could still go with all of us."

"It's not like you don't *know* our fathers," said Margaret. "You've been around them forever."

"I know," I said. "But I just don't want to. It wouldn't be the same."

"We could dress Brian as a grownup and let him escort you," said Ellen.

"*Orrr*," said Amy, drawing out the word. "Hey, everybody, I've got this terrific idea. How about *Zachary*? How about getting Zachary to take Tottie to the father-daughter dinner?"

"ZACHARY?" I screamed so loud that Fang stopped sniffing whatever he was sniffing and turned to growl at me. "Zachary? Zachary? *Zachary*? Zachary's the reason I can't go in the first place." I moved away from them over to the curb, and sat down, pulling my knees tight against my chest. "I can't believe you said that."

"But you said . . . about your dad having to go to the medical thing . . . And what's that got to do with Zachary?" Amy sputtered as she spoke. She sat next to me while the other two stood in front.

"It was a lie," I said.

"I don't get it," said Ellen. "I mean, does your father have to go to a meeting?"

"Is there even a meeting to go to?" said Margaret.

"And what's any of that got to do with Zachary?" said Amy, reaching over to touch me on the arm.

"My father doesn't have to go to any meeting because there isn't one, and we're not going to the dinner because I'm not telling him about it and you'd better not either. And it's still all Zachary's fault."

A car came down the street and Margaret and Ellen moved in closer so that I was staring at their knees and breathing Fang's dog breath. The car passed and they stepped back as Margaret said, "I'm not sure I get it, but what's any of this got to do with Zachary?"

"It's because of Zachary that I don't know if I can like my father anymore. It's because of Zachary that I keep giving my father hairy eyeballs and don't want to talk to him. It's because of Zachary that my father's not exactly the person I thought he was."

"But why because of Zachary?" said Amy. "What did he do?"

"He got born," I said.

"Yeah?" said Ellen.

"Yeah," said Amy. "I get it. Because for Zachary to get born, your dad and his mother had to . . . you know . . ."

"Don't say it," I said.

"But that was a long time ago," said Margaret, "and he's still Dr. Flannigan and is so incredibly nice. He came to see me every day I was in the hospital when I had my appendix out and he didn't even have to because he was just the pediatrician and not the surgeon who was actually in charge."

"Everybody does stuff a long time ago. We will—I mean we haven't yet, but we will—and then ages from now it will have been a long time ago and people will forget and not hold it against us," said Ellen, joining Amy and me on the curb. "Like my mom, before she married my father, was married to somebody else and nobody still thinks she was an idiot for once being married to an abusive creep."

"And my dad got arrested for drunk driving the night of his senior prom, and my grandparents freaked out and wouldn't let him drive for about a million years even after the law said he could, and they sent him for counseling and everything. Now he's Mr. Straight-and-Narrow, and if he has so much as a glass of wine he makes my mom drive," said Margaret as she shortened Fang's leash and went to sit on the other side of Ellen.

"Yeah," said Amy. "And I wet my pants the first day of kindergarten and there was pee all over the floor and eventually people forgot. Because it was a long time ago."

"Zachary was a long time ago," I said, "and during all those years my father didn't know where he was, and he even went and wrote that book, *Kids First*."

"But he thought Zachary was *adopted*, you even *told* us that," said Amy and Margaret and Ellen more or less at the same time.

"And besides, your dad's not a mind reader," said Margaret. "What'd you expect?"

I pushed my legs out in front, then drew them in again. I thought about Ellen's mother and Margaret's father and about Amy wetting her pants in kindergarten. "Yeah, I guess," I said. "But I'm still not going to the dinner. And this cement is getting really cold, so let's move on."

Of course my mother found out about the father-daughter dinner. Call it ESP or whatever you want, but she tracked me down in the basement one day when I was looking for my purple T-shirt in the laundry room. "I hear the dinner's next week. Did you get a check from your father or what? And what are you going to wear? That blue dress is probably getting a little short and—"

"I'm not going," I said as I fished the shirt out of the dryer.

"Not going?"

"Nope. It's sort of a drag and I don't feel like it this year," I said.

She gave me one of those long steady looks, and I could tell there were all kinds of things piling up in her head waiting to be said. I stared down at the broken tile on the floor, studying the zigzag edges, determined not to say anything more. After what seemed like hours, my mother sighed. "Suit yourself," she said as she turned and went upstairs.

The father-daughter dinner was on a Friday night of what will probably go down in history as one of the most boring days of my life. Once school was over, everybody rushed home—to iron dresses, get haircuts, take showers, wash hair, curl hair, and (Ellen even said this) paint their toenails. As if they were all going barefoot to the dinner.

When I got to my house, there was nothing to do but a whole weekend's worth of homework right then on a Friday afternoon, which is pretty much against my principles. And to make things worse, Brian's dorkiest friend—a really weird kid named George—arrived just before supper, complete with sleeping bag. The whole time we were eating, Brian and George giggled and snorted and made disgusting animal noises which, for some inexplicable reason, my parents thought were funny.

"You're only encouraging them," I said, giving everyone at the table a withering look.

"Lighten up a bit, Tottie," my mother actually said. "They're just having fun."

When we'd finished eating and the dishes were done, Zachary, who never goes anywhere, went out. The two seven-year-old creeps took over the TV and the VCR to watch *Shrek*, which I'm convinced they'd each seen 750 times already. My father went off to his den to do some work and listen to the ball game, and Mom curled up on the living-room couch with her nose in a book. Which left me, with nothing to do.

There was no one to call. The TV had been taken captive. I didn't *feel* like reading and I hated solitaire. I tried to do the crossword puzzle in the morning paper but couldn't and ended up jamming it into the recycling bag. I thought about sending all my friends instant messages, but nobody would be home to receive them, so I filled Punch's bowl with fresh water instead. I put it down on the mat, but somehow it didn't look full enough, so I did it again. And again. When I found myself filling that stupid bowl for the fourth time, I grabbed my sweatshirt and a basketball and went outside.

It was the kind of warm, still night that made me think spring might really be coming someday. I dribbled my way around the driveway, pretending I had hold of Zachary Pearce's head each time I bounced the ball. I made a couple of jump shots, then moved back by the garbage cans to practice foul shots. I tried a layup and missed and had to fish the Zachary-head out of the brier bushes. I shot from the right of the basket, and then the left, then the right again, sort of lulling myself with the thud of the ball. I don't know how long I'd been doing this when the kitchen door opened and my father came out.

"Want some company?" he said. "Want some competition?"

"I guess," I said, tossing him the ball.

After that things really picked up mainly because if my father hadn't been a pediatrician, he could've been a basketball player. Not Michael Jordan, but a basketball player anyway. I mean he was fast and his arms were about two miles long and always seemed to be waving in front of me, no matter where I was when I tried to shoot. The air seemed to echo with the sound of the ball swooshing through the net.

"Good one," Dad yelled when I sank an almost hook shot. I retrieved the ball and handed it to him before going over to collapse on the steps. He kept shooting by himself a while longer, then came over and sat beside me. "Nice night, huh?"

"Yeah," I said. "Like maybe it's really spring."

We didn't say anything after that but just sat, listening to a siren somewhere in the distance and to Mrs. Batterton's ugly dog barking to be let in. It was funny sitting there like that. Even though there was no conversation holding us together, I didn't quite feel that I could just get up and leave. I was still trying to figure out why, when my father said, "Well, I guess they're having the chocolate marshmallow sundaes about now, don't you think?"

I froze. I couldn't speak, or even swallow.

"Tottie?"

"You knew?" I managed to croak.

"Yes, I figured it was about time and I did a little investigating. And when you didn't mention it, I decided that you had your reasons for not wanting to go this year . . ."

I didn't say anything and my father finally went on. "And that those reasons probably had to do with me and Zachary, and what it was like to suddenly have this stranger living in your house who is your father's son, and how hard it must be to find out that maybe your father isn't the person you thought he was."

Oh wow. Right then I decided that in addition to being a pediatrician and a basketball player, Dad could have been a mind reader. That it wasn't just mothers who had ESP.

"And maybe this was a good year to skip the dinner," my father added.

"Yeah, maybe. I guess."

"And I also realize that it's probably very hard to go from being the special older child to being in the middle of two brothers. Yes?"

Up until that minute I hadn't thought of it that way—but my father was right. Now, if I said yes, it'd be admitting what a wormy small-minded person I was. And if I said no, it'd be a lie.

"They say that hindsight is twenty-twenty," Dad said, when he figured out I wasn't going to answer. "And looking back, I'm so incredibly wise. Looking back, it's perfectly obvious that I should have investigated to make sure the baby really was given up for adoption and, I'm not sure about this, maybe even told you about the child. Looking back, I can't believe I didn't realize that it was within the realm of possibility that even a child who'd been adopted could show up one day. Sooner rather than later. And wrong as I know I was, I can't right that wrong by turning my back on Zachary now. Can you see that?"

He reached for my hand, and when he squeezed my fingers I squeezed his back. Which, I guess, was some kind of answer. After a minute he stood and pulled me up beside him. "There's some S'mores ice cream in the freezer, and while it's not exactly a chocolate marshmallow sundae, it's pretty close. How about it?"

Zachary

I've been thinking about my mom a lot lately. Not that I ever *don't* think about her, but still, in the last couple of weeks it's been a lot. I guess that's because of this whole gardening thing and the fact that I've been spending so much time in the yard, raking and just generally mucking out the flower beds.

If there was one thing my mother always wanted, it was a garden. "Just you wait . . ." she used to say. "When we get a house of our own . . ." She read flower catalogues in winter, and had it all planned, with peonies ("they have a certain boldness, Zach") and zinnias ("easy to grow . . .") and daisies ("because I like them"). Maybe even a tree. I'm not remotely sure about these things, but I half hope that, wherever she is now, she can see me out there, doing my Mr. Green Jeans routine.

The other day the doctor said that it was almost time for the first grass-cutting of the season. I said I'd do it. He said they had a service. I said I'd *be* the service. He thought a minute and said okay, and that if I edged and trimmed, he'd pay me what he used to pay Doug. And that if I wanted to look for any more jobs in the neighborhood, I could use his mower. I said, "Yeah" and "Thanks" and "That'd be great."

And afterward, it occurred to me that we'd just had a conversation.

The money part was a real plus and would, I figured, go a long way in solving my financial problem. Until then, Winnie had been doling out funds for a soda at lunch and bus fare and some extra, but I didn't feel right taking it. She always said to let her or the doctor know if I needed cash, but I never could, and a couple of times, when Jordan and Tom and some of the other guys from school asked me to do stuff on weekends, I'd turned them down. With one lame excuse after the other.

After the doctor and I made our arrangements, the backyard pretty much became my domain. Mine and Punch's and sometimes Brian's. And Mrs. Batterton's, from the other side of the fence. Mrs. Batterton claims dominion over the whole neighborhood, or so it seems.

Brian calls her Mrs. Battle-ax behind her back, and Tottie, in a rare display of half-sisterly concern, warned me about her a day or so after I got here. I don't have a real firm opinion of her yet, but if she's on Tottie's hate list, she might be an okay person.

Another reason I'm thinking about my mom so much lately is that my stuff arrived from Ohio. I really have to hand it to the doctor. I mean, I don't know how he did it—but he did. It was all there: the things I asked for, and even some I didn't but found I needed anyway.

I unpacked the boxes in the kitchen with Brian's help, and the weird part was, no matter how much I wanted to tell him to bug off, having him there kind of helped. He kept up a steady stream of "What's this?" and "Where'd you get that?" which helped dilute the sadness I seemed to be wading through. And afterward, he helped me carry a lot up to my room.

I cleared a place in a bookcase for the stereo and after a bunch of wrong moves managed to get my computer up and running. I shoved clothes into drawers, books onto shelves, and set a picture of my mother and me out on the dresser. Then I stood back, giving everything the once-over and thinking how the room was on its way to look-ing like my own private space.

We had left the TV from home on the kitchen floor,

which turned out to be a good thing because if I'd lugged it upstairs, I'd have had to turn around and lug it down again. "Sorry, Zach," Winnie said. "Dave and I have always had a rule about no TVs in the bedrooms." She stopped for a minute, remembering, I guess, the nineteen-inch in her and the doctor's room. "No TVs in the *kids'* rooms, anyway. But there is that extra room in the basement with that old couch and a couple of chairs in it. How would that do?"

It actually did just fine and turned out to be an okay place to hang out. Trouble was, Brian liked it, too. And Punch. And even Tottie, from time to time. There wasn't much I could say, though. I mean, hey, they were giving me a house. It was the least I could do.

Life at Xavier was still the best part of this whole Baltimore deal. It was too late in the year to join anything, but some of the guys I'd been hanging around with were serious lacrosse nuts, and I was beginning to pick up the game, more or less by osmosis. The other night, Jordan's father had a bunch of extra tickets for an Orioles game at Camden Yards, and Tom and I and a couple of others got to go along. It was my first major-league experience since I was eight, when Mr. Reynolds took me to a Reds game. The O's lost—but it was still exciting.

When I got home that night, Tottie and her father were

in the kitchen eating ice cream. "How was it?" the doctor wanted to know. "I listened to the first few innings on the radio, but then Tottie and I got involved in a little one on one and came in for ice cream. Want some?"

It was as if I'd never had the hot dog and soda Jordan's dad had sprung for at the stadium, because I was suddenly ravenous. I went to the refrigerator, fixed myself a bowl, and sat down, filling the doctor in on the rest of the game. "The O's were doing great through the seventh inning, but then the pitching totally fell apart and the Yankees took over," I said.

"Yeah, we've been known to have trouble with the Yankees that way," he said. "I'll try to get tickets for some night once school is out and we can all go."

Just then, Winnie came into the room. She asked about the game, too, and we went through the whole Yankee thing again. She asked what I thought of the stadium and a bunch of other stuff. And for a while, we all, except for Tottie, sat there talking. Almost like real people.

I could tell by the look on Tottie's face that this wasn't high on her list of things to do. But she hung in there. She didn't bolt.

Tottie

"It doesn't seem even a little bit normal," I said. It was Friday afternoon and my mother and I were on our way to the orthodontist, where I was to have a checkup *and* explain to Dr. Heraldson how I had lost my retainer for the second time. Brian was home with Zachary, which just might possibly be the only good thing about Zachary—he makes my life with Brian less concentrated.

"What doesn't?" said Mom.

"The way you actually *like* having him here."

"Him who?"

"Zachary."

"Give it up, Tottie," my mother said, as she pulled out from behind a stop sign. "First you went through that whole he's-not-who-he-says-he-is routine and—"

"I *know* he's who he says he is now—I just don't *want* to know it. And I don't understand why you never even got mad and just let him move in."

"How many times are we going to have to go over this?" Mom asked. When I didn't answer, she sat through a whole red-light cycle before adding, "Besides, I *was* mad."

"How come you never showed it then? How come you were all sweetness and light, making him turkey-and-ham sandwiches and putting clean sheets on his bed?"

"Remember how I told you that first night that I wanted to want to do what was right? I just kept trying to hang on to that idea, and anyway, I was never quite sure who I was mad *at*. But you never saw me at the health club those first few days. I pedaled that stationary bike hard enough to have gone to Philadelphia and back, and I got the treadmill going so fast I could barely keep up."

"You never thought about leaving, though, did you? You know, going off to make a whole new life the way Valerie Marsden's mother did in fourth grade—and all her father did was bring home twin Great Dane puppies." The weird thing was that I hadn't known I was worried about my mother maybe leaving until I asked the question, and then I got all quaky inside waiting for her answer.

"Leave? Me? Good heavens, no."

"Did you want Dad to leave? Or Zachary?"

"I certainly didn't want your father to leave. And as for Zach, I have to confess to wanting him not to have come—but once he was here I never wanted him to leave." Mom turned onto the parking lot in front of Dr. Heraldson's office. "Besides," she went on, "you know that your father told me about the child back when we first started getting serious about each other. But after that, it wasn't something we discussed much through the years, though I realize now that he must've thought about it more than I knew. In case you don't know it, your dad doesn't always let on to what he is thinking. Somehow I knew, that first Saturday afternoon, that Zachary belonged with us. Now come along, let's not keep Dr. Heraldson waiting."

All the time Dr. Heraldson was poking and gouging and doing whatever orthodontists do, I lay back in the chair and thought how that whole conversation hadn't gone the way I'd hoped it would. I mean, impossible as it may sound, I think I still had some wild idea about getting my mother to turn against Zachary, and that maybe the two of us could conspire to get rid of him, to send him back to Ohio or on to Texas or someplace. Which, as I stared past Dr. Heraldson's head at a wisp of dust dangling from the ceiling, I realized wasn't going to happen.

"Well, Tottie, your mother tells me we need to order you another retainer," said Dr. Heraldson, giving something a final look, then quickly taking his hands out of my mouth. Which led me to think that someone might actually have had the nerve to bite him once. "I must say I got quite a kick out of that piece she wrote the *last* time you lost one. Quite a kick."

I waited till we had made the next appointment and were out of the office and in the car, before I told my mother about my idea. "You know how the last time I lost my retainer you wrote a column about it that Dr. Heraldson thought was an absolute riot?"

"A lot of people did," said Mom. "I got an incredible response to that piece, but if you recall, it wasn't just about you and your retainer. It was about all the stuff we'd lost in the family around that time—Dad's favorite screwdriver, Brian's sneakers, my glasses, and the wooden picture frame that used to sit on the bookcase in the living room."

"All Dr. Heraldson remembers is the retainer," I said. "But anyway, what I was thinking was, since you've already got *one* column out of my retainer, if you have any plans to write another about *this* one, then you ought to pay me for supplying you with the idea—and then I'll have the money to pay for the new retainer. Okay?"

"Wrong," said my mother as she pulled into the driveway. "The way I look at it, ideas are there for the taking, just wafting on air, as it were. But I will help you to get money for the retainer—the cellar needs a good cleaning, including the furnace room. And that'll go a long way toward paying off your debt."

Paying off your debt. The words rang in my head all the rest of the afternoon and through dinner as my father and Zachary carried on a conversation about lawn care, which only made me think how unfair life actually is. I mean, there's Zachary setting up his own grass-cutting business that he's going to get paid *money* for, while all I get is to clean the gross old basement for credit toward a *retainer.*

Aside from the unfairness of it all, grass cutting didn't really interest me and I began to space out, thinking about how Mr. Weinberg in art class talked about "patterns in art and life." He showed a bunch of slides of ancient pots and vases, Native-American designs, and present-day tile floors and porch railings. Then he gave us our assignment—to find a pattern that "spoke to us" and copy it onto a sheet of 15-inch-wide drawing paper. I was thinking how art isn't exactly my thing, but also about Mom's Hopi necklace she got in Santa Fe and the way the design on it seems to be a series of wind gusts and lightning bolts, when my father's voice yanked me back to the dinner-table conversation.

"Did you have a driver's license in Ohio, Zachary?" I heard him say.

"No, I never did. I was about to get my learner's permit, and then my mother had an accident. It wasn't her fault, but this exterminator truck ran a stop sign and . . . well, the car was totaled and . . ." Zachary shrugged, waiting a moment before he went on. "And not long after that, things started getting worse—with her health—and there—we— So I never did."

"I'm sorry," Dad said, and I wasn't sure whether he meant about the monster exterminator truck or Susan Pearce's illness or what. "But I think once school's out for the summer, we'd better sign you up for driver's ed," he added. "What d'you think?"

"Cool," said Zachary.

"I'll second that," my mother said. "It'll be a big help having an extra driver in the family."

Oh, swell, I thought. *Now he'll get the job of driving me and my friends around, and they'll be fawning all over him as if he were somebody really special.* "He's from Ohio and he won't know where anything is," I said.

"Well, Tottie, you'll just have to be the navigator," said my father, winking at me as if we shared some secret joke.

I was still dealing with the driving business when I heard Zachary say, "Mrs. Batterton asked me to take over her yard work for the summer, and you'll never believe her list of rules. First pooper-scoop the yard, then keep the grass a half-inch longer on the front lawn than on the back, cut the backyard first so Toby can watch through the fence while I do the front, and a whole bunch of other stuff."

"Hmmmmnn," my father replied.

"Mrs. Battle-ax? *That* Mrs. Batterton?" asked Brian.

"That Mrs. Batterton, and Brian, I've told you not to call her that," said Mom.

"And Mr. Abel from across the street said he'd pay me twenty dollars a week to do his lawn," said Zachary.

"That sounds fair," said Dad. "But make sure you charge Mrs. Batterton at least that much—her yard's a little larger, and there is the matter of pooper-scooping. Work out the details with her ahead of time. Always discuss money up front."

"Well, yeah," said Zachary. "I did that already, and she said okay."

Double swell, I thought, as I sat listening to all this. *My non-brother, the entrepreneur.*

Zachary

It's not that I'm a total cynic, but when things go too well, I get suspicious. The bomb's going to drop, the other shoe's going to fall, the safety net in the circus is going to give way. It's nothing new, and back when I was a kid, I remember Grandma sometimes calling me a Gloomy Gus, a crapehanger, or a killjoy, then reaching to give me one of those bone-crunching hugs she specialized in.

"Lighten up," Mom would say, on more than one occasion. "We've got the world by the tail. What can happen?"

The answer to that is *plenty*. And it did.

But it's the here and now that's bugging me. I mean, after I dealt with what had to be dealt with in Ohio, I took that flying leap (courtesy of Greyhound) and landed in Cleaver heaven. What's spooking me now is that the Cleavers are pretty much turning into regular people. Which is definitely unsettling.

Take Brian, for instance. He's really into chess, and for his age, he's amazing—enough so that I really have to pay attention to the games. But more than that, I like to think I'm teaching him the fine art of conversation, unless the whole concept of Motormouth as conversationalist is a walking oxymoron. Anyway, he's catching on to the whole *I*-talk-and-*you*-listen-and-then-*you*-talk-and-*I*-listen thing. Except when he's with a bunch of other seven-year-olds, and then all bets are off.

Then there's Winnie, a really okay lady. Even so, she's the one who's hardest to figure, and I can't help wondering what she had to say that first day, when the doctor got home and she told him I was there. And what she says now, in their room with the door closed. The thing is, she seems so incredibly accepting that I want to believe that what I see is what there is.

She showed me a bunch of her old columns the other day—some funny, some sad, and some sort of in-between. A lot about the family, all in an okay way, but I'll bet anything my appearing on the doorstep'll never make it into print. Not even Winnie's that cool, or that crazy.

What's to say about the father? Well, for starters, he's coming out from under his rock more often. Literal translation: he's spending less and less time in his den reading medical journals and wishing I'd disappear. Another thing—he hands me the sports page from time to time, saying stuff like, "The O's have picked up a new catcher who looks promising." Or, "Hey, read this, Zach. It'll go a long way to explaining why lacrosse is such a big deal around here."

He's pushing driver's ed for the summer. Then late the other night, when I'd just settled down to watch *Psycho*, he came and sat on the other end of the couch, putting a bowl of popcorn on the cushion between us. After that, like regular people, we watched TV and ate popcorn, all the way down to those unpopped kernels at the bottom of the bowl.

The Cleaver update wouldn't be complete without Tottie, though. The worm in the apple—that's Tottie in spades. Which is okay by me because it keeps things on the up-and-up, keeps them from being too good. And for a genuine Gloomy Gus, that's important.

None of that's kept me from trying to figure her out, though. In fact, I've even tried to do that walking in the other guy's shoes that Mom used to talk about. If I were Tottie and she were me—how would it be?

Or say I'm me, back in Ohio, and Tottie shows up at the door and then she and my mother are into this long-lost-daughter routine.

Then what? Would it be all right? And could I deal with it?

And the answer is—I don't know. I honestly don't know.

Tottie

If this is spring, I'll take something else. Something warm and dry, where your feet don't squish through slime every time you go outside and Mom doesn't sing the "Take Those Shoes Off and Leave Them by the Door" blues nonstop. Add to that the fact that it's been cold and seriously gray and has rained or almost rained every day for a week. *And*, it's the week of spring break.

Some other years we've gone away—to the beach a lot, and another time to Washington, D.C., where we took a tour of the White House and went to the top of *their* Washington Monument and even stayed in a hotel, though we live only an hour away. And once we went to New York City. This year we didn't go anywhere because one of the other doctors in my father's office had already made plans to be out of town.

So there we were, enjoying what my father called "a rampant epidemic of cabin fever." Trouble was, he always said that as he made his escape to the office and the cases of tonsillitis and strep and chicken pox waiting for him there. Mom did her regular mother stuff and then headed up to her workroom, where she was writing a "light and amusingly provocative" column on science projects. When I told her there was nothing light *or* amusingly provocative about science projects, she just smiled and went in and closed the door. I'll bet anything she was sending E-mails to her friends and maybe even reading a novel instead of working on her article. At least that's what I'd be doing.

Zachary spent a lot of time up on the third floor, which is now known as Zachary'sthirdfloor, as if it were all one word. He also went out some with a couple of guys named Jordan and Tom who are so okay I can't figure what they're doing with him. Brian and his friends were what you might call equal-opportunity annoyers, dragging their slickers and muddy shoes from one house to another.

As for me—Ellen, Margaret, Amy, and I went to the movies twice, the mall once, and to lunch at the museum with Margaret's grandmother once. We spent the rest of the time on the phone or sending IMs, trying not to think about Katie Jones, whose entire family went to Jamaica for the *week*.

The rain stopped sometime Thursday night, and the sun was out full blast on Friday. This immediately sent Zachary into full eager-beaver mode with the Great Grass-Cutting Business. He cut a lawn across the street and one around the corner. Then, after two somewhat frantic calls from Mrs. Batterton, he headed over to do hers.

"Poor Zach, I hope he hasn't bitten off more than he can chew," said Mom, watching out the window as he unlatched Mrs. Batterton's gate and pushed the mower into the yard.

"Yeah, poor Zachary," I said as sarcastically as I dared. Then I headed downstairs to put in more retainer time on the basement.

By Saturday, though, the rain was back and I was seriously bummed. Another problem was that Margaret and I were supposed to get together here to work on our art projects, but at the last minute her mother wanted her to go along when they took her grandmother to the airport. And by the time she called to tell me all this, the entire rest of *my* family had left. Not that I would have wanted to go to College Park to sit in the rain and watch lacrosse with Dad and Brian and Zachary. No way. But Mom had gone to the mall to, as she put it, revive her spring wardrobe. Which would've been sure to include a stop at the Gap or Old Navy for me.

So there I was. Home alone. Bored out of my mind. I poked around for a bit, watched a couple of cartoons and an old *Gilligan's Island* on cable, and then decided to get started on my art project. I found Mom's Hopi necklace in her top drawer where she always kept it and took it into my room, lining it up on the desk along with the india ink and the special pen Mr. Weinberg had lent me. I hadn't remembered to ask if I could borrow the necklace, but I knew my mother wouldn't care. She's one of those people who think school projects are super-important.

The whole project turned out to be tons harder than I expected. The problem with a repeated pattern is that you have to keep *repeating* it. And every time you do, it's supposed to look exactly like it did before. I kept at it, though. At least until my fingers started to cramp and the muscles in my back felt as if they were on fire. I put my pen down, unscrunched my hands, and got up to move around.

The house was creepily silent. Even Punch, who was

sleeping in my parents' room, just looked at me and closed his eyes again when I tried to get him to play. For want of something better to do, I scooped up a pile of blankets Mom had put on the third-floor steps, carried them upstairs, and shoved them into the hall cupboard where they belonged. And then, instead of coming back down, I found myself in Zachary's room. Almost as if my feet had taken me there on their own.

I stood for a minute, looking around but not quite sure what I expected to find. I mean, by now I knew he was who he said he was, but still . . . A part of me hoped. Maybe there was a secret journal, filled with deep dark secrets. Things my father should know, that only *I* could tell him about. But first I had to find them.

The weird thing was that, although he didn't have a ton of stuff, the room had a definite Zachary stamp on it. There were a couple of shirts draped over a chair, schoolbooks spread on top of the desk, a watch and a handful of change and a thing of deodorant on the dresser, and a picture of him and a woman I took to be Susan Pearce in a wooden frame. I checked out his stereo and his collection of CDs, and even looked at the book on his bedside table. Overall the room had kind of a boy smell, too, like Brian's only different—sort of like the insides of closets.

I can't believe what I did next, and the whole time I was

doing it I felt really crummy. But I did it anyway. I peered under the bed and felt around between the mattress and the box spring, not quite sure what I was looking for. Then I tiptoed over to the dresser, pulling out the drawers one at a time, sifting through the tangle of socks and underwear and T-shirts. There were a few more pictures of Susan Pearce and one of Zachary when he was about ten, holding a soccer ball. There was the letter we'd all seen, the one his mother had written telling him where to find his father. *My* father. But other than that, nothing, and I stood there for a minute feeling cheated. And creepy for being there.

Just then the phone rang and offered me an escape. I tore down the stairs and into my parents' room, picked up the receiver, and gasped, "Hello."

"It's me," said Margaret. "We're back from the airport, so why don't you come over now, and Mom says you can stay for dinner. Only it's getting late, so let's not work on our projects today. Okay?"

"Yeah, great," I said. "Besides, I already worked on mine some and my back's never going to be the same. Anyway, I'll be right over."

Back in my room, I shoved Mom's necklace into my desk drawer, closed up the india ink, and put my project on the top of my bookcase, out of harm's—and Brian's—

way. Then I wrote a note telling Mom where I'd gone and left it on the kitchen counter.

Margaret's family must have been suffering from cabin fever, too, because the minute it stopped raining late in the afternoon, her father dragged the patio furniture out of the garage and announced that we were having the first cookout of the season. He put the two of us to work with a spray bottle of 409 and a bunch of paper towels while he fired up the grill and Margaret's mom brought out pasta salad and regular salad and ketchup and mustard and three kinds of pickles.

It wasn't *exactly* warm enough for a cookout, but with sweatshirts and windbreakers, none of us really cared. It was just good to finally be outside. And when we got *really* cold, Margaret's mother brought out hot chocolate, and we sat holding the steaming mugs, trying not to notice that our teeth were chattering.

Zachary

I knew something was wrong as soon as Winnie came down to start supper, but she waited until we all (minus Tottie, who was at some friend's house) sat down to eat before letting on what it was.

"My necklace is missing," she said, putting her hand up to her chest, as if it might suddenly have reappeared.

"Which necklace?" the father asked.

"The Hopi one. My good one, you know, that we got in Santa Fe. I wanted to see how it looked with the green shirt I bought today and when I went to get it, it was missing."

"Did you look?" the father said. "Maybe you put it in some other place." He reached for a piece of bread, as satisfied as if he'd just solved the *New York Times* crossword puzzle with his eyes shut.

"Of course I looked," said Winnie. There was a sting in her voice that made me suddenly not hungry. "And besides, I know *exactly* where I put it. Where I *always* put it."

"Don't look at me," said Brian. "I don't even like necklaces."

Don't look at me, I wanted to say, but the words stuck in my throat.

"I'm sure there's an explanation," the father put in. "We'll look again after supper."

That's when the whole dining room turned into some sub-zero terrain. A silent one. That's when my food turned to sawdust and I knew if I ate it I would gag. Without looking at her, I was somehow sure that Winnie was looking at me. That little worms of suspicion were crawling through her head, and that she was exchanging meaningful glances with the father. Glances that almost shrieked, "Something like this was sure to happen. What did you expect?"

I didn't do it, I wanted to shout over and over. *I didn't do it.* And the worst part was that, except for me, nobody knew instinctively that I hadn't done it. The way my mom would've.

I'll never forget the time when I was eight and Sammy Boylin told my mother that I'd thrown his best Batman action figure into the stream behind his house and now it was gone forever. Mom knelt down, eye level with Sammy, and told him straight off that she knew I hadn't done that and she'd like him to think very hard and see if he could remember what really happened. That's when old Sammy totally lost it and started blubbering, with snot running down his face and onto his red jacket. He shook his head and said he'd broken Batman himself, trying to fit him into a hole in a fallen tree, and was afraid to tell his mother. Mom wiped Sammy's face, snot and all, and said she'd go with him and help explain to his mother that sometimes things just broke.

Later that night I asked her how she'd been so sure I hadn't done what Sammy said I'd done. "Because that would have been a mean thing to do, and while you may get into your fair share of trouble, Zach, I know you're not mean," is what she said.

But here, nobody *really* knows me. Or what I would and wouldn't do.

Upstairs in my room once dinner was over, I began to think again about leaving—which, I have to confess, I hadn't considered lately. Mostly, I guess, because I'd gotten complacent. Because I'd been lulled by life at Xavier, by Brian and Winnie and the way the father no longer looked at a spot a couple of feet from where I was standing when he talked to me. And maybe by this whole family thing. I thought about today, and the lacrosse game at College Park, and about the father and whether, if push came to shove, he might stand up for me. But why should he? What had I ever been to him?

See, I told myself, *things really were going too well.*

I wondered if I should wait for them to accuse me—or just go now.

All these thoughts plus not having eaten dinner eventually gave me a headache, and I went down to the kitchen to look for food. I was sitting there at the table finishing a meat-loaf sandwich and a glass of milk when Tottie came in the back door.

"Hi," she said. "What's up?"

I shrugged and shook my head, and then, almost without meaning to, I said, "Your mom's upset. She lost her necklace."

Tottie

I should have said it right out, as soon as Zachary mentioned my mother's necklace. I should have said I had it, that it was in my desk drawer, in my room. *Should've—* but *didn't.*

Instead, I took off up the stairs, stopping to say good night to my father. I knocked on the bathroom door to let my mother, who was taking a shower, know that I was home. Then I went into my room and closed the door, feeling a giant balloon of excitement growing inside of me.

I grabbed my nightshirt, dug out the lilac bubble bath Amy had given me for my birthday, and headed into the bathroom I share with Brian, locking the door into his room. After that, I ran the water in the tub as high as it would go without actually sloshing over and got in, lying back and letting the bubbles creep under my chin. And all the while I was pretending I was in one of those humongous pink marble bathrooms you see in magazines instead of our plain old bathroom where the tub is just a tub and everything is white. I kept holding off my thoughts, the way I do with the last piece of candy in a box, until they finally broke through and spun around me and I found myself smiling up at the ceiling.

My mother's necklace was missing. Her favorite one. And I had it. I knew I should return it that very minute, but maybe, just maybe, if I didn't—if I managed to really lose it—then my mother and father would both think that Zachary had taken it. Which would make him a thief. And if Zachary was a thief, my parents certainly wouldn't want him in the house anymore. And they'd have to admit I'd been right all along. *And* he'd have to go. Maybe to the cousins in Texas, or back to Ohio. After that we could get on with being a regular family, the way we'd been before.

I smiled at the ceiling again. I stayed there like that, grinning and soaking, till the water started getting cool and the bubbles faded. Then I drained the tub and stood up and took a shower, because I've never figured out how you're supposed to wash your hair in a bubble bath. Even a lilac one.

Back in my room, I climbed into bed with a book, but as soon as I started to read, more thoughts skittered across the page. Would my mother call the police? Her necklace wasn't all that valuable, but would she? Would we have some kind of big farewell for Zachary, taking him to the bus station or the airport, or would he go quietly, the way he had come? Would Brian miss him? How about my father—would he feel he'd lost something he'd just recently found? One thing, though. Mom'd be glad to see him go—the kid my father had had with some other woman. *Except*, I was almost 100 percent sure my mother really *liked* Zachary.

I tried to concentrate, but my book had suddenly turned boring, right there in the middle of chapter seven. My pillow was damp from my wet hair and felt cold and clammy. My stomach hurt. There was something big and heavy inside my chest that hurt when I breathed. I sat on the edge of my bed, staring down at my toes and thinking about Zachary Pearce and the way he'd looked all streaky-gray when I'd seen him on my way through the kitchen. As if he already knew what might happen.

I grabbed the blanket off the bed and wrapped it around me. But even so, I shivered and my stomach hurt more than it had before. The thing in my chest grew even larger. *They don't have to know, and if I keep my mouth shut they'll probably just send him away,* I thought, expecting to feel better than I did. I tried to smile, but my face was a board. I tried to swallow, but couldn't.

My room seemed suddenly smaller than it ever had before, as if the walls were pushing in. When I tried to say anything out loud, the words froze. Then, after a very long time, I got up, pulled the blanket even tighter around me, took the necklace out of the drawer, and went across the hall to my parents' room.

"I have your necklace," I said, holding it out to my mother. "We have this project for art, all about patterns in art and life and we were supposed to find some design we liked and then copy it. Only you weren't home this afternoon so I borrowed the necklace, because of the Hopi design, and then when Margaret called I just shoved it in my drawer and forgot about it. Till Zachary told me it was missing."

"Oh, thank heavens," my mom said. "I've torn this dresser apart—I knew it had to be here someplace."

"You mean you didn't think Zachary had taken it?" I asked, my voice suddenly small and squeaky.

"Of course I didn't think Zachary had taken it. Any

more than I thought you or Brian or your father had taken it," Mom said. "To tell the truth, I was beginning to think I was losing my mind—that I'd put the necklace in a strange place and just forgotten about it. Like the time I put my car keys in the refrigerator and the butter on the windowsill."

"And I was thinking we'd all have to go back to Santa Fe, so we could replace it," my father said with a laugh.

The trouble was, if I thought by giving my mother's necklace back I'd suddenly feel fine, I was wrong. My stomach hurt just as much as it had before and the thing in my chest was growing, growing, growing.

I moved over and sat on the edge of the bed. "There's something else," I said. "Something I have to tell you."

Mom settled onto her side of the bed, pushing the pillows up in back, and Dad sat on the rocker across the room. "What is it, Tottie?" he said.

For a minute I couldn't say anything and sat looking from one to the other.

"Tottie?" said Mom.

"I didn't want to tell you. About the necklace, I mean. I didn't want to tell you and I wanted to never give it back because then I was sure you'd think Zachary really did take it and then you'd send him away and we'd go back to being the way we were before." The words came spilling out into the room and sort of hung there, surrounded by silence.

"I see," my father said after a while.

"I wanted all that to happen," I went on. "But then the more I wanted it, the more I felt really rotten. And besides, I remembered how Zachary looked, all gray and funny, when I came in and he told me the necklace was missing. Almost like he *knew* that's what people were thinking. That he was a thief."

"Oh no," my mother said, getting up off the bed. "Zach was very quiet at dinner, but do you think he really did believe we thought he'd taken it, Dave? We've got to tell him right now that Tottie had the necklace all along. That we never, not in a million years, thought he was a thief."

My father stood up and headed for the door, but before he opened it he turned to me and said, "One thing, Tottie. This *is* the shape of our family now. A mother, a father, a daughter, and two sons. Got it?"

Zachary

The father called me to come downstairs. Was this the great banishment scene waiting to happen? I wondered. Would they dump my belongings on the front walk or, more likely, would we have some totally civilized parting of the ways? Some keep-in-touch or let-us-know-next-time-you're-in-town kind of thing.

"Zach," he called again. "We'll be in the kitchen."

Which is where I found them, except for Brian, drinking milk and eating cookies. Only Tottie looked like maybe her cookie was made of rotten fish—or else the milk was sour.

"We're celebrating—I found my necklace," said Winnie. "Tottie had it for some art project and just dropped it into her desk drawer when she went out. I figured there had to be some logical explanation and it was driving me crazy not knowing what it was. And Zach, I'd feel awful if I thought in any way that you'd gotten the impression I was accusing you, because that never entered my mind. So if you did—think that . . ."

"No, it's cool," I said. Then a giant wave of relief washed over me and I knew no way had I wanted to leave.

"I wanted them to think you took it," said Tottie, her voice sounding tight and strangled.

"Tottie!" said Winnie. "What—"

But my father held his hand up to make Winnie stop, and shook his head.

"I wanted them to think you took it—to think you *stole* it. That's because, when I got home from Margaret's and you were sitting at the kitchen table looking all gray and funny, I knew that's what *you* were thinking. That that's what *they* thought." Tottie stopped for a minute and then, before anyone else could say anything, went on.

"I thought about that when I went upstairs. How instead of taking the stupid necklace out of my drawer I could just lose it permanently, and they'd think you took it, and after that they'd realize they didn't know all that much about you so why should they bother to keep you here. And they'd send you away."

I didn't want to listen to her anymore. I didn't want to

look at her face with its I-smell-something-really-rotten expression. Right then I felt the way I had when I was six and was standing at the end of the diving board at the Y trying to get up enough nerve to jump. And I did what I did that other day—closed my eyes and took the plunge.

"What do you think it was like for me?" I said. "Coming into this *Leave It to Beaver* house."

"Gross," said Tottie, curling her lip.

"You didn't really think we were like that?" said Winnie.

"I did—but I don't now. But still, it's not that I mean this to sound ungrateful, and you were all cool about taking me in and letting me stay, and about the school and everything, but not one of you know what it was like for me to have to come here that day. Not one of you ever asked. Not one of you know who I really am—I am who I say I am, but I mean on the inside."

My voice rose and I couldn't get it under control. "After that first day, not one of you wanted to know anything about me or my mother or what our life was like before, and while I'll always appreciate what you've done, it's still like you *put* me in your family instead of ever trying to *fit* me in. And then tonight, with that whole necklace thing, I did figure you thought I'd done it. And that would be your excuse to get me out of here."

"I'm really sorry you thought that tonight," said Winnie. "But what I'm having trouble figuring out is why you —or Tottie—thought that if you did something wrong, you'd be out of here. That's not the way it works in a family." She got up and went to stand in front of the sink, leaning back against it. "There's something you have to understand, Zach. I don't think you have any idea how complete a shock it was the day you showed up at our door. Though I knew, just by looking at you, who you were. There was so much to be dealt with on such short notice—how to be fair to you and, at the same time, explain all this to Tottie and Brian. How to tell David, when he came in from the office, because we were both so sure you had been adopted. I had some issues of my own to deal with, too. The fact that you were David's son whom he'd had with another woman, telling myself that I wanted to do what was right for all of us, and feeling my way to finding what the right thing was. But your being you made it easier because we all took to you right away, and though I guess I was wrong here, I thought you were starting to fit in."

"I didn't," Tottie said. "I didn't take to you right away. I didn't even know you existed, and then all of a sudden— *pow*—an instant brother, and an older one at that. Then there was Brian who thought you were really cool, and all my friends who kept saying they felt sorry for you, and *my* mother being super-human nice, and nobody seemed to care what I thought, especially about my father and some woman having a *baby*. And there you were, settling into the third floor and going to Xavier and on outings with *our* grandparents, and I didn't ever want you to fit in, and a lot of times I wanted you to leave. But maybe now I guess I know it wasn't so much *you* I didn't like, but more the idea of you."

The weird thing was, everything she said made sense. But before I got to tell her so, Tottie went on.

"And then tonight, I was sure I had my chance to make you disappear. But then, the more I thought about it, the worse I felt. I mean, totally rotten. And that's when I knew for sure that I didn't really want you to leave."

The room was suddenly quiet. I looked over at Tottie and sort of nodded. She looked at me and sort of nodded back.

"My turn, I guess," my father said. "You know, Zach, all these years I've thought about when you might come looking for me, when you were older. And then you were here, and there was no chance to get ready, no more time to think, and there I was face-to-face with the lives that were about to be affected by what I'd done. With the people I'd somehow cheated or might be about to cheat. And still, like Winnie, wanting to do what was right."

"I wasn't cheated." I spit the words out in a spray of saliva. "Mom and I had a great life. It was terrific, just the two of us until . . ."

"Until Susan died," he said. "Now let me say just this one thing, in case I've never made it clear enough. I'm glad you're here—but I'm sorry your mother had to die to make it happen."

The conversation went on, between Winnie and Tottie and my father and me. Our voices rose and fell. The cookies got eaten up. After a while we heard a *thump-thump-thump* on the stairs and Brian was there, in the doorway.

"I was asleep and you woke me up," he said. "You guys talk too much."

He turned and went back upstairs, and the rest of us looked at where he'd been, and laughed.

Tottie

It was the morning of the Fourth of July when my mother
came downstairs with several typed copies of *the column*.
All of us were sitting around the kitchen table, which had
turned out not to be as crowded as we'd once thought, especially if we squished. She propped the pages up between
the strawberry jam and the rack of paper napkins.

"I know some of you have had mixed feelings about my
writing this. In fact, there've even been some dire warn-
ings," she said, looking right at me. "But I've tried to be
careful, and I'd like everybody's input before I send it in to
my editor."

We each took a copy, even Brian, whose reading usually
consists of chapter books about mummies and dinosaurs

and hidden treasures. After that, things got quiet for a few minutes, except for the *plink, plink, plink* of water dripping in the sink and the rustle of paper.

"No," I said, when I'd read the last line of the last page. "No, no, no."

"It's yucky, Mom, and not like real people," said Brian. And I suddenly thought there might be some hope for him as both a brother and a human.

"That's not exactly it," said Zachary, putting his copy on the table and then picking it up again, as if it might have changed while he wasn't looking.

My father hesitated for a minute, and I knew he was being careful because my mom can be really sensitive about her writing even when she *says* she wants the truth. He finally cleared his throat and said, "Well, Winnie, maybe a little more work—"

"You think it's not quite right?" said Mom. "Well, does anyone have a suggestion?"

I thought right off of saying *Don't write it,* but was pretty sure that wasn't what our last year's English teacher meant when he talked about constructive criticism. "It's just that—it's just that it's sickeningly nicey-nice and doesn't sound anything like our family. Besides, it's not even *true*—the way you described what went on when Zachary came to live here," I said all in a rush.

"It's yucky," said Brian, "and somebody might read it and think we were really like that." Brian was shaping up right before my eyes.

"I guess I see what you're trying to do, but it doesn't feel completely honest. But that's just my opinion," said Zachary.

"Maybe if you could show us, warts and all," said Dad, reaching over to squeeze my mother's hand.

"But," said Mom, "I wasn't sure how much—whether to be—"

"Yucky," said Brian, taking the last half bagel out of the basket.

"*If* you're really going to write it—which, of course, you could just *not* do—you've got to tell it the way it really was," I said, figuring I was positively stacking up points for constructive criticism.

"Warts," said Dad.

"Honesty," said Zachary. "*If*, as Tottie says, you're really going to write it."

"I'd like to," said Mom. "It was such an important thing—when Zachary came to live here—the problems and the way we all felt. And it's a part of all of us."

"Then write it that way," said Dad. "You can do that better than anyone I know."

My father had five tickets to an Orioles game that afternoon, but Mom stayed home to work on her column. Margaret got to go in her place, which was good because she likes baseball about as much as I do, which meant I'd have someone to talk to.

My mother probably knew in her head that the first Zachary column was off, and even knew how to fix it. By the time we got home, she had a bunch of copies of the revised version lined up on the kitchen counter, plus she had made chicken salad and had brownies in the oven.

I wasn't sure I wanted to read this latest version, and then once I'd read it, I wasn't sure if I was happy or sad. There was a prickly feeling in the backs of my eyes, and I had trouble swallowing. But it was all there—how hard it must've been for Zachary to come to us and how hard it was for us, in our different ways, to have him there, and how we're finally learning to be a family. "Warts and all," I said. "But it's—okay. Better than okay."

"Good," said Brian, heading for the backyard.

Zachary nodded, and my father went over and wrapped his arms around my mother and held her tight.

My mother's column ran the next week, and thirteen people called that day to say they liked it, as did the teller at the bank and the produce man at Eddie's. To tell the truth, I still felt a little creepy, knowing our family was out there for the whole world, or at least the people in Baltimore, to read about. And I couldn't help wondering what she was going to do next.

The following Saturday Dad took Zachary, Brian, and me to a bookstore to help him select a birthday present for my mother. While he and Brian were in the music department, Zach and I pawed over the table of new releases, picking up one book and then another, and putting them all back. We had already rejected gardening books, cookbooks, historical novels, and science fiction when we spotted *the* book at the exact same second, both of us reaching out, both of us saying, "Yes!"

"It's what I've always thought she should do," I said. "And it'd keep her really busy."

"And she might not have as much time for the column anymore," said Zach, looking at me and nodding.

We pooled our money, took the book home and wrapped it in newspaper, and put it with the presents Dad had bought and the one Nanny and Granddad had sent from North Carolina and something from Brian in a blue plastic grocery bag. That night we went to Café Zen for dinner and came home for ice cream and cake.

"Save ours for last," I said when it was time for Mom to open her presents.

"Okay," she said, and then went into her shaking-and-pinching-and-feeling-the-presents-all-over routine before she finally opened the CDs of all gazillion of Haydn's London Symphonies from Dad, and the abandoned bird's nest from Brian, and the yellow cotton sweater from my grandparents. "And now, what could this be?" she said, shaking, pinching, and feeling all over again.

"Come on, Mom," I said.

"Yeah, Winnie, come on," said Zach.

"O-kay," my mother said as she tore the paper off and sat looking down at the book. "Okay." A giant smile crept across her face as she held up the book called *How to Write the Novel You've Always Wanted to Write*.

"Is this what you two think I should do?" she asked.

"You could try," I said.

"It's worth considering," said Zach.

"I just might do that," Mom said. "Thank you both so much, and I just might do that."

Zachary

It was the day after Winnie's birthday, and I was in the yard hacking at some monster bush that was running amok and thinking about the column she'd written. The one where she talked about my coming to live with them and how, as a family, we were still a work in progress. In a way, reading it had been a real bummer for me—a lot like taking a big gulp of too-sour lemonade and then finding the sugar at the bottom. It made me feel totally weird when Tom and Jordan and a couple of the other guys said they'd read it. But the thumbs-up, way-to-go letter from Father Connor really helped. I even saved it.

I stepped back and looked at the bush and had just moved in to attack the other side, when Tottie came out.

"Hey," she said.

"Hey. Hot enough for you?"

"Yeah, but I like it this way, especially since I'm going to the pool with Amy and Margaret. But anyway, she's reading it."

"Amy? Margaret? Reading what?" I said.

"No, Mom. She's reading the book we gave her. I checked the bookmark and she's up to chapter six already and has written notations."

"Promising," I said. "And I meant to tell you, when I came in last night and said hi, she just looked up and mumbled something about plot structure and dénouement. Which is a good sign. And just think, once Winnie actually gets started on the novel she's always wanted to write, or *we* want her to write—well, the possibilities are endless. You think?"

"I think," Tottie said. She started back to the house, then stopped, turning to say, "Yeah, well I almost forgot. Dad's looking for you—something about those shelves he's putting in. Anyway, he's in the basement."

I headed down the cellar steps, feeling the cool air rising up to meet me and the words taking shape in my head. "Hey, Dad," I called. "Tottie said you were looking for me."